A terrifying message . . .

"I want my baby back!"

Amanda stood staring into the mirror above the sink. She didn't want to believe what she was seeing. Someone had written the words on the steamy mirror.

Terrified, Amanda spun around.

No one was there.

Her imagination was playing tricks on her, Amanda hoped. When she turned back to the mirror, the only thing she would see would be her own reflection.

But the words were still there.

"I want my baby back!"

Grave Secrets

A. G. Cascone

For Elise—
the baby sister we look up to—
for everything . . .
for always

Copyright © 1997 by Annette Cascone and Gina Cascone.

Cover art copyright © 1997 by Broeck Steadman.

Published by Troll Communications L.L.C.

Deadtime Stories is a trademark of Annette Cascone and Gina Cascone.

Printed in the United States of America.

10 9 8 7 6 5 4 3 2 1

CHAPTER 1

There was no stopping what was about to happen, and Amanda Peterson knew it. Even as she watched Jared Clark and Kevin Stewart racing toward the back of the yard, she knew it was hopeless.

"Noooooooooo!" Amanda's best friend, Laura Baxter, cried out in terror. But it was too late.

Amanda had hit a home run. But Amanda didn't run the bases, or do a victory dance, or even smile. She just stood there frozen, watching in horror as the ball she'd just smacked sailed over her back fence into the yard of the house that stood at 704 Shadow Lane.

Amanda gulped. The ball game was definitely over.

"I'm out of here," Laura announced, dropping her glove.

"Oh, no, you don't!" Amanda caught Laura by the back

of her shirt as she tried to escape. Laura always bugged out at the first sign of trouble.

"I am not going over there to get that ball," Laura said, shaking her head adamantly. "I don't care what you say. I'm not doing it. So don't even ask me."

Like anybody would ask her, Amanda thought. She loved her best friend, but Laura was definitely not the kind of person you sent on a life-or-death mission.

"I wasn't going to ask you to go," Amanda assured her. "I'm going to go. I just don't want you to leave me by myself, in case something terrible happens." Amanda released her grip on Laura. "I wouldn't leave *you*," she added deliberately, turning and heading for the back fence. Laura followed a moment later, just as Amanda knew she would.

Jared and Kevin were peering intently through the gap where a section of the Petersons' fence had come loose from the post. "It's not good," Jared said gravely as he stepped back so Amanda could see for herself.

Peeking through the crack in the fence was like peeking into Dr. Frankenstein's yard. Even in the middle of the afternoon, the property at 704 Shadow Lane was dark and eerie. The enormous old trees in the back of the yard blocked out the sun completely. And the ancient gray stone house loomed in the shadows, gloomy and foreboding. The windows were hung with heavy draperies, except for the basement windows, which were covered with grime and thick iron bars.

The only thing scarier than the house at 704 Shadow

Lane was the old woman who lived inside it.

"Over there." Kevin pointed to where Amanda's ball had landed. "Right next to the shed where she throws the rats after she bites their heads off."

Amanda shuddered. Biting the heads off rats was just one of the horrible things old Mrs. Barns liked to do.

"No way your ball is lying in Barnsey's dead rat pile!" Laura cried.

"You'd just better hope those rats are all dead," Kevin told Amanda.

"Of course they're all dead," Laura snapped. "They don't have any heads!"

"Maybe the ones in the pile are dead," Kevin informed them. "But their brothers and sisters are still running around that yard. Listen," he added, "you can probably hear them squeaking."

Amanda couldn't hear anything but the sound of her own heart beating.

"If I were you," Jared finally spoke up, "I'd forget about going in there after that ball."

"She can't," Laura shrieked, horrified by the suggestion. "What if Barnsey gets her evil old hands on it? What happens then? Huh?"

"Probably the same thing that happened to that Lizard kid," Kevin answered.

"What lizard kid?" Jared asked.

"The Lizard kid," Kevin repeated impatiently. "You know, the kid who blew up in his own front yard."

It was an old story, one that had been handed down

over so many years, there was no one around who had actually seen it happen. But all the kids still believed it had.

"*Lu*zard," Jared corrected him.

"Lizard, Luzard, who cares." Kevin rolled his eyes in exasperation. "The kid's still dead, isn't he? And all because Barnsey got her hands on something that belonged to him."

It was a water pistol. At least that's the way Amanda had heard it. And while there were several other variations of the story, one thing was certain. There really had been a Frederick Luzard. And now he really was dead. Amanda and her friends had seen his tombstone in the cemetery. He was eleven-and-a-half years old when he died.

The same age as me, Amanda thought with a shiver.

"Nobody really knows what happened to that kid," Jared said.

"Cut me a break." Kevin was not about to drop the subject. He was scared to death of Mrs. Barns and took every opportunity to spread the fear around. "Everybody knows what happened to that kid. He burned up just like that!" Kevin snapped his fingers. "Barnsey put a spell on him, and the kid fried."

"It's too awful to even think about." Laura cringed.

"Yeah, well, think about what she did to Todd French!" Kevin said.

Todd French was the only person they actually knew who claimed to have suffered under an evil spell cast by

8

Mrs. Barns. It all started the day after one of his brothers tossed Todd's baseball cap onto Barnsey's property to see if Todd was brave enough to go get it. But he didn't go, and according to Todd, that was the worst decision of his life.

"Barnsey did not put a spell on Todd French," Jared insisted.

"Oh, yeah?" Kevin shot back. "Then how do you explain the twenty-seven stitches he got in his head the day after Barnsey got his cap?"

"It was nine," Jared corrected him. "And he walked into the sliding doors at the supermarket."

"Because Barnsey made him," Kevin insisted. "And a week later, she made six of his teeth fall out."

"No, the dentist had to pull two of his molars out to make room for the rest of those buck teeth he's got," Jared said.

"And what about the lice?" Kevin asked.

Amanda was waiting for the logical explanation. But even Jared seemed to be stumped by the lice.

"Todd French does not have a spell on him," Jared finally huffed. "Besides, he's still alive, isn't he?"

"For now," Kevin said ominously, looking directly at Amanda.

"You can't let Barnsey get her hands on that ball." Laura pointed out what Amanda already knew.

Amanda wasn't entirely convinced that Todd French was suffering at the hands of Mrs. Barns, but she didn't want to take any chances. "I've got to go get it," she announced. Before she could change her mind, she started to squeeze through the fence.

"No." Jared stopped her. "I'll go."

"Let Jared go, Amanda." Laura jumped on the offer. "He can run faster than anybody."

Amanda really wanted to let Jared go in her place. But she couldn't. If Jared messed up and Barnsey got her hands on that ball, Amanda would be the one to fry for it anyway. "I've got to do it," Amanda told Jared. "It's my ball."

She could tell by the look on Jared's face that he was relieved she'd let him off the hook. Amanda knew Jared would have gone in her place if she asked him to. He was always trying to prove to the rest of them that they didn't have to be so scared of Barnsey. But she was sure that, deep down, Jared was every bit as scared as she was.

"Just don't let her catch you," Kevin warned, "or you'll end up in her dungeon with that other little girl."

The dungeon was Barnsey's basement. It was where she tortured all of her victims—before she finally buried them.

"Why don't you just shut up?" Jared glared at Kevin. "There is no little girl."

"Is too," Kevin insisted. "She's been down there for months."

"How do you know that?" Jared asked.

"Because Todd French said he saw her looking through the bars on those windows just before he ran away," Kevin informed him.

"Oh, brother," Jared sighed. "Todd French can't see his own two feet without those new goggle glasses he wears."

"Well, he saw the little girl," Kevin declared. "And he said that she was all bloody and stuff."

Amanda could see the panic on Laura's face as she turned back toward the fence. If Amanda was going to do this, she had to do it now, before she chickened out.

"Keep your fingers crossed," Amanda told the rest of them. "And watch out for Barnsey. If she sees me, I'm dead."

Amanda took a deep breath. As she squeezed through the gap in the fence, she could feel her heart pounding all the way down to her fingertips. She focused her eyes on the ball.

It's not so far away, she told herself. Amanda was a fast runner, almost as fast as Jared. She could be there and back in less than a minute. *It's going to be okay,* Amanda assured herself. *I know I can make it.*

"Go," Jared urged her, peeking through the gap from the safe side of the fence. "Fast!"

As Amanda tore off, she heard Kevin calling after her. "Watch out for the rats!"

Rats! She'd forgotten all about the rats! But there was no stopping now. Besides, rats, even ones without their heads, were a whole lot less terrifying to Amanda than the thought of Barnsey getting her hands on that ball. Still, she watched the ground carefully, praying that she wouldn't step on anything, dead or alive.

Amanda made it to the shed without spotting a single furry, fanged creature. The ball was lying right near the open door. There were no headless rats piled around it. But as she bent down to grab the ball, she heard something moving around inside the shed.

Amanda's heart stopped. What if the rats were in there? Or worse yet, what if it was Barnsey? What if Barnsey was waiting to grab her and take her to the dungeon with the other little girl she had locked up down there?

Amanda grabbed the ball and took off, running fast enough to break Olympic records. She looked back only once. No one was behind her. Ahead of her, and coming closer fast, was the fence. She could see the amazement on her friends' faces. Just a few more feet and Amanda was home free!

"Move!" Amanda ordered the rest of them as she hit the fence hard. "Get out of the way!"

Jared, Kevin, and Laura stepped back to make room for Amanda to squeeze through.

"You did it!" Laura congratulated.

"I can't believe it!" Kevin chimed in. "You really made it!"

But Amanda was only halfway through the fence when she felt icy, skeletal fingers clamp down on her wrist, as cold and as inescapable as handcuffs.

*"N**ooooooooo!!!!"* Amanda screamed as she felt the bony fingers tighten around her wrist.

She was halfway back into the safety of her own yard! But now she wasn't going to make it the rest of the way!

"Where do you think you're going?" Barnsey's voice croaked.

"Help me!" Amanda shouted frantically to her friends. "Don't let her take me to the dungeon!"

Jared had already grasped her other arm and was pulling as hard as he could without hurting her. Kevin grabbed on to Jared and started pulling him. And Laura held on to Kevin. It was like a giant tug-of-war.

For a scrawny old woman, Barnsey seemed to have superhuman strength. She was holding Amanda in a death grip from which there seemed to be no escape.

"Oh, I don't think I'll bring you to the dungeon,"

Barnsey cackled. "Maybe I'll just drag you over to the shed and bite your head off!"

They shrieked in terror as they struggled frantically to pull Amanda free. As they tugged with every ounce of strength that each one of them could muster, Barnsey suddenly released Amanda's wrist. The four of them toppled over like dominoes. But they'd barely touched the ground before they were up and running. They didn't stop until they reached the back door of Amanda's house. Only then did they turn to look behind them.

Luckily, Barnsey hadn't followed them. She wasn't even watching through the fence.

"That was a close call," Jared gasped, doubling over to catch his breath.

"Way too close," Kevin agreed.

"I thought I was a goner." Amanda had to struggle to hold back tears. She'd never been so terrified in her life. It had barely sunk in that it was over and she was safe.

"How did Barnsey get you?" Laura asked. "Didn't you see her out there?"

"Didn't you?" Amanda shot back. "You guys were supposed to be looking out for me!"

"We were," Jared assured her. "But I never saw her coming."

"Me neither." Kevin backed him up. "It's like she appeared out of nowhere."

"It's because she's a witch," Laura said. "She's got all kinds of evil powers we don't even know about."

"She does not," Jared argued.

"Then how did she just appear like that?" Amanda demanded.

"I don't know." Jared shook his head in frustration.

"Maybe she was there all the time, and we just didn't see her because she was hiding behind a tree. There are lots of trees back there big enough for her to hide behind."

"Maybe." Amanda shrugged. She wished she could believe that Jared was right about Barnsey. But after what had just happened, it was getting more difficult.

"Besides," Jared continued, "what difference does it make now? You got the ball, and you made it back in one piece."

Amanda hadn't even thought about that. She looked at the baseball in her hand and laughed in relief. But when she tried to toss it up into the air, her fingers wouldn't let go. She'd been clutching it so hard that her fingers had gone numb.

Jared gently pried it from her hand. "You're pretty brave," he told her.

"Not really," Amanda admitted. "I was scared to death the whole time. Especially when Barnsey grabbed me." Amanda rubbed her wrist, trying to forget how Barnsey's fingers had felt when they were wrapped around it. Then her heart started to pound. "Oh, no!" Amanda cried.

"What it is?" Laura asked.

"My bracelet!" Amanda held out the wrist she'd been rubbing. "It's gone! I've lost my bracelet!"

"Your friendship bracelet?" Laura touched her own bracelet, the one that matched Amanda's. "Are you sure?"

"It's gone!" Amanda's voice rose in dismay.

"Are you sure you were wearing it?" Jared asked.

Amanda nodded. "What if I lost it in Barnsey's yard? Or what if she ripped it off my wrist while she was holding on to me?"

"Oh, man," Kevin said, staring wide-eyed at Amanda. "If Barnsey's got your bracelet, you're doomed! She's going to put a curse on you, just like Todd French."

"Shut up, Kevin," Jared warned. "You probably just lost it while we were playing ball," he said to Amanda. "I bet it's right here in your own yard."

Jared didn't wait for anybody to agree or disagree with him. He just started looking for the bracelet.

The rest of them followed his lead. There was nothing else they could do.

The grass was high, too high to be able to spot something as small as a bracelet easily. So they got on their hands and knees and combed the lawn carefully, inch by inch.

Amanda prayed that Jared was right, that if they searched long enough and hard enough, they would find her bracelet. *Think positive,* she told herself as she ran her fingers through the grass.

Amanda's face was so close to the ground, she didn't see what was ahead of her—not until she found herself face-to-face with something so awful, the scream stuck in her throat.

CHAPTER 3

When Amanda finally managed to scream, it was loud and shrill and seemed to go on forever. Her friends raced to her side.

Laura gasped the moment she saw what Amanda was screaming about.

"Oh, gross," Jared groaned as he pulled Amanda to her feet.

Kevin didn't flinch. In fact, he bent down to take a closer look. "This guy's been dead for a while," he announced, nudging the dead squirrel with the toe of his sneaker. "He's already got like riga-morphasis and all. You see?" Kevin nudged the squirrel again. "He's as hard as a rock."

"It's *rigor mortis,* you idiot," Jared corrected him. "And I don't want to see."

"Poor little guy," Amanda said, brushing herself off.

"What do you think happened to him?"

"I don't know," Jared told her. "Maybe he was just old."

"Or maybe he fell out of a tree," Laura added, offering her own explanation.

"Squirrels don't just fall out of trees," Kevin said.

"Oh, yeah?" Laura shot back. "Well, maybe this one did."

"Or maybe somebody killed him," Kevin suggested ominously.

Laura laughed. "That's so stupid," she told Kevin. "Who would kill a squirrel?"

Kevin turned his head to look at Barnsey's house. And Laura stopped laughing immediately.

"Cut it out, Kevin," Jared scolded before Kevin could open his mouth. "Barnsey did not kill this squirrel."

"Oh, yeah?" Kevin opened it anyway. "Well, maybe she did!"

"For what?" Jared asked impatiently.

"Yeah," Laura chimed in, nervously. "For what?"

"I don't know," Kevin said. "Maybe she was going to eat him or something."

"Everybody knows she eats rats," Laura reminded him. "Not squirrels."

"Yeah, well, maybe she's sick of rats," Kevin went on. "I mean, how many rats can a person eat? Or maybe she was just going to have him for dessert."

"Oh, brother," Jared huffed. "If Barnsey wanted to eat this squirrel, what's he doing over here?"

Amanda didn't believe for a second that Barnsey was going to eat the squirrel for dessert. Or even for dinner, for that matter. In fact, she was beginning to think the whole conversation was pretty funny. Until Kevin finally spit out his response.

"Maybe she threw him over here to send us a message," Kevin told them.

"What kind of message?" Laura asked, wide-eyed.

"A bad one," Kevin answered. "Like if she catches us in her yard again, we're going end up just like him!" Kevin pointed at the dead squirrel.

"There's something seriously wrong with you," Jared said to Kevin, exasperated. "The poor little thing just died back here, that's all. Mrs. Barns did not kill him. And she is *not* trying to send us a message."

Amanda wanted to believe that with all her heart. The problem was, Mrs. Barns really had threatened to drag Amanda to the shed and bite her head off. Maybe Kevin wasn't as crazy as Jared thought he was.

"Yeah, well, I'd be praying really hard that we find your bracelet on this side of the fence," Kevin told Amanda. "Because Barnsey doesn't even have to catch you to kill you!"

Laura went pale. And so did Amanda.

"Are you just stupid?" Jared asked Kevin. "Or are you a *real* moron? Mrs. Barns has never killed anybody. And she's not going to, either!"

"Oh, yeah?" Kevin shot back. "Why don't you try telling that to the Lizard kid!"

"Just shut up, Kevin!" Amanda finally snapped. Kevin was working her into such a terrified state, she couldn't take it anymore.

Jared was right. Mrs. Barns hadn't killed anybody, and she wasn't going to, either, Amanda told herself. As she tried to calm her fears, Amanda also told herself that the bracelet had to be somewhere in her own backyard. She'd lost it while playing ball, and sooner or later it would turn up. She was sure of it. Well . . . *almost* sure of it.

"Yeah, Kevin," Jared agreed with Amanda. "Why don't you just shut up."

"Fine," Kevin snapped. "My lips are sealed." Kevin turned the imaginary key to lock his lips shut. But he wasn't silent for even a second before he added another comment. "Just like his!" Kevin nudged the dead squirrel with his foot again.

Amanda shook her head at him in disgust.

"So what do you want to do with the squirrel?" Jared asked Amanda.

"I guess we should bury him," Amanda answered.

"I say we chuck him back into Barnsey's yard," Kevin chimed in.

"That's mean," Laura told him. "This poor little squirrel doesn't deserve that. Even if Barnsey did throw him over here."

"We're going to bury him," Jared insisted. "It's the right thing to do."

Amanda sent Laura into the garage to get a shovel, while she ran into the house to find a shoe box big enough to hold the body. By the time the two of them returned with the shovel and squirrel coffin in hand, Kevin and Jared were in the back of the yard, looking for an appropriate burial plot.

"How about we put him here?" Jared suggested, stepping on a piece of ground about a foot from the fence.

"No," Amanda told him. "That's too close to Ralph." Ralph was Amanda's pet hamster. But he hadn't been her pet for long. Two weeks after Amanda got him, Ralph had died. "See." Amanda pointed to a rock next to Jared's foot. "That's his tombstone." The stone was covered with dirt, but the name "Ralph" was still visible, written in red felt-tipped marker.

"How about here?" Jared stepped on another spot.

Amanda shook her head. "I think Herman is there."

"Who's Herman?" Laura asked.

"My goldfish," Amanda reminded her. "Remember?"

"Oh, right." Laura nodded.

"While you guys are picking out a plot," Kevin snapped impatiently, "why don't you give me the coffin, and I'll go get the diseased."

"Deceased," Jared corrected him.

"Whatever." Kevin grabbed the shoe box from Amanda and headed off to get the squirrel.

It took at least another fifteen minutes to find a spot by the fence in the "pet cemetery" that wasn't occupied. When they finally moved past Snitch the canary's grave, Jared grabbed the shovel and started to dig.

The ground was hard, and Amanda could see that Jared was having a difficult time. The shovel hit one stone after another. As Amanda stood there watching him, she hoped she hadn't picked a cemetery plot that was already being used by another dear departed pet she'd forgotten about. In fact, Amanda was hoping that the shovel wouldn't hit anything else at all.

But it did—and Amanda's heart came to a total and complete stop.

From under the earth where Jared was digging came a faint, muffled sound. It wasn't just a sound, Amanda realized with alarm. It was a voice. A voice that cried *"Ma-ma!"*

There was definitely a grave under their feet—and Amanda was sure it wasn't a pet's.

CHAPTER 4

"Did you hear that?" Amanda gasped.

"It sounded like a baby," Laura said nervously.

"Yeah, well, you'd better hope it's not a baby," Kevin told her. "Because that sound came from that hole! And if it is a baby, then somebody buried it back here."

"It's not a baby," Jared assured them. "Who would bury a baby in Amanda's backyard?"

Kevin started to answer.

But Jared cut him off. "Don't even say Barnsey."

"Well, if it's not a baby, then what is it?" Laura asked.

"I don't know. But I'm going to find out." Jared lifted the shovel and was about to drive it into the ground again.

"Don't!" Amanda stopped him. "What if it is a baby?"

"It's not a baby!" Jared shouted. But he dropped the shovel anyway and got down on his knees to dig with his hands.

Kevin joined in. But Amanda and Laura stood back.

"What is it?" Amanda demanded the second Jared stopped digging. She didn't want to see for herself—not until she was sure it wasn't something awful. She'd already had more than enough scares for one day.

"It's just a stupid doll," Kevin answered, sounding disappointed. He tossed it out of the hole, and it landed at Amanda's feet.

Amanda and Laura bent down to inspect the doll more closely while Jared and Kevin continued the work of burying the squirrel.

"It sure is ugly," Laura said.

Amanda was forced to agree. If the doll had ever been pretty, she showed no signs of it now. Her clothes were filthy, tattered, and worm-eaten. The hair was matted, and it stuck straight up from the top of her head. Amanda could tell that it used to be blond, but now it was mostly muddy brown. The doll's face was dirty and scratched. One blue eye was open, and the other was caked shut with dirt. It was obvious that the doll had been in the ground a long, long time.

"Where do suppose she came from?" Amanda asked.

"From in the hole," Kevin said over his shoulder as he put the squirrel coffin in where the doll had been.

"I mean, who put her there?" Amanda rolled her eyes at Kevin's stupidity.

"Didn't you?" Laura asked.

"No," Amanda told her. "I'd never bury one of my dolls. That's way too creepy—kind of like burying a person."

It had been a long time since Amanda had actually played with dolls, although she did have an enormous collection of them. They were fine, porcelain dolls that

Amanda's mother began collecting for her from the time she was born. By the time she was ten, Amanda had so many dolls that her father had to build extra shelves above her bed so she could display all of them.

"Maybe Casey did it," Jared suggested, as he began to cover the squirrel coffin with dirt.

Casey was Amanda's little sister. She was only five years old and she still played with dolls. But she didn't play with them very nicely. Casey didn't own a single doll that still had all its body parts. She'd colored on them, tattooed them, and butchered their hair with her safety scissors. It was entirely possible that Casey had played funeral with them as well.

Amanda picked the doll up off the ground. She held it with two fingers and looked it over closely. She wanted to make sure that there were no bugs on it, no slugs or centipedes. When she was satisfied that there weren't, she started brushing off the dirt.

"No way Casey buried this," she told the rest of them. "Look at it. This doll is really, really old. Whoever buried it did it a long, long time ago."

"Maybe it was the people who lived here before you," Kevin suggested.

"Nobody lived here before us," Amanda reminded him. "We moved into this house when it was brand-new. This whole backyard was nothing but woods before our house was built."

"That means somebody buried this doll in the woods," Laura said. "Now, that's really creepy."

"What's so creepy about it?" Jared laughed. "It's just a doll."

But there *was* something creepy about it. At least Amanda thought there was. It was even creepier when she squeezed the doll's cloth body in her hands and nothing happened.

A chill ran up Amanda's spine. "How did this doll say 'Mama'?" she asked her friends, knowing that even Jared wouldn't have a logical explanation after he heard what she said next. "It doesn't have a voice box!"

CHAPTER 5

"Give me that thing," Kevin said, grabbing the doll from Amanda's hands. First he looked it over. Then he squeezed it a couple of times. Next he banged it against his leg. But no sound came from the doll.

"See," Amanda said. "I told you it doesn't have a voice box!"

Laura's eyes were wide with fear. "Then how did it say 'Mama'?"

"Maybe it's haunted," Kevin shrieked, dropping the doll onto the ground.

Amanda knew that Kevin was just trying to scare them, and she didn't appreciate it. She was already scared to death. "Knock it off," she shouted at him.

Kevin burst out laughing. "Gotcha!"

"You don't really think this doll is haunted, do you?" Jared asked Amanda as he dumped the last shovelful of dirt on top of the squirrel's grave.

That was *exactly* what Amanda thought. What else was there to think? "It doesn't have a voice box," Amanda repeated, speaking very slowly, as if Jared were a complete idiot.

"The voice box must have fallen out in the hole," Jared replied, speaking to Amanda as if she were an even bigger idiot.

Of course! Amanda thought. She felt pretty stupid as she bent down to pick up the doll.

"You guys are such suckers," Kevin taunted them.

"And you're a real jerk," Laura shot back. "Besides, I still think that doll is creepy."

Amanda was about to agree when her mother appeared at the back door to call her in for dinner.

As her friends left the yard through the side gate, Amanda headed across the patio toward the house with the doll still in her hands. She thought about bringing it inside to show to her parents, but then she decided that wasn't a very good idea. Her mother would probably yell at her for bringing something that dirty into the house. So she set the doll down on the picnic table before she went in.

Amanda realized she'd made the right decision the minute she started telling her parents about the doll.

"Please tell me you didn't bring that thing into the house," her mother said as she sat down at the dinner table.

"No," Amanda assured her. "I left her outside on the picnic table."

"I want to see her." Casey hopped up from the table and started out of the room.

Amanda's father stuck out his arm and caught Casey

28

before she could make it past him. "Oh, no, you don't." He laughed. "It's dinnertime, pal."

Casey plunked herself back down in her seat.

"So what are you planning to do with this doll?" Amanda's mother asked.

"I don't know." Amanda shrugged. "She's in pretty bad shape."

"Maybe you ought to just throw her in the trash," her mother suggested hopefully.

Amanda knew that was probably what she would end up doing. But somehow that seemed even worse than burying her. "Don't you think it's weird that someone buried a doll on our property?" Amanda asked her parents.

"Well, it hasn't always been our property," Amanda's father pointed out.

"I know," Amanda told him. "It wasn't anybody's property before we moved in. It was just woods."

"It was all just woods," her father agreed. "But some of the property actually belonged to Mrs. Barns."

"Mrs. Barns?" Amanda gasped. That was the last thing she needed to hear.

"Yes." Her father chuckled. "Mrs. Barns. Don't you remember what happened when we put up the fence?"

Amanda shook her head no.

"Sure you do," her father said. "It was a terrible mess. The guys who put up the fence built it two feet beyond our property line, right in Mrs. Barns's backyard. We would have had to move the whole thing if Mrs. Barns hadn't been so nice about it. Luckily, she just offered to sell us the last couple of feet of her property so that we could leave the fence where it was."

"So the doll we dug up wasn't really buried in our backyard at all?" Amanda asked with alarm. "It was buried in Barnsey's backyard?"

"Amanda," her mother reprimanded. "How many times have I told you not to call Mrs. Barns that? It's not nice."

Amanda was too upset to even pretend to be sorry.

"Does it really make a difference whose backyard the doll was buried in?" Mr. Peterson asked.

Amanda knew that if she answered that question honestly, she'd just be in for another lecture about "poor old Mrs. Barns."

Amanda's parents thought that all the stories about Mrs. Barns were nothing but nonsense. They insisted that Mrs. Barns was so tormented by the neighborhood kids that she only pretended to be mean and scary so that she could keep the constant harassment at a safe distance. They even felt sorry for Mrs. Barns. They said that she was just a "lonely old lady who didn't have any family or friends."

Kevin had tried to convince Amanda's parents that maybe the reason Mrs. Barns was "a lonely old lady" was because she'd *buried* her family and friends in her own backyard—after she'd tortured them in her dungeon. But Mr. and Mrs. Peterson didn't want to hear about it. And they definitely didn't want Amanda repeating it, particularly in front of Casey.

Still, Amanda couldn't help wondering if maybe Kevin was right, especially now.

Maybe Barnsey's friends aren't buried in her backyard! Amanda thought with a gulp. *Maybe they're buried in mine!*

The idea hit Amanda so hard, she nearly choked on her chicken.

"Amanda," her mother reacted. "Are you okay?"

Amanda nodded yes, while her brain kept screaming no.

"Here," Mr. Peterson said, handing Amanda her glass. "Take a sip of water."

Amanda did as she was told. But it wasn't a piece of chicken sliding down the wrong pipe that had Amanda gasping for air. It was Barnsey.

She didn't say so, but the answer to her father's question was "yes." Digging up that doll from Barnsey's backyard did make a difference—all the difference in the world.

CHAPTER 6

By the time Amanda went to bed, she had worked herself into such a state that she couldn't fall asleep. As she lay there in the dark, quiet room, with nothing to distract her, Amanda's imagination began to run wild.

What if Barnsey really did have her bracelet? What if she was down in her dungeon right now, putting some horrible spell on Amanda?

Amanda pulled the covers more tightly around her, but still she didn't feel safe.

Maybe Laura is right, Amanda thought. *Maybe Barnsey really is some kind of a witch. Maybe she's rubbing my bracelet right now so that she can get me to sleepwalk right down to her dungeon. Then she can torture me before she buries me in my own backyard!*

"Stop it!" Amanda told herself out loud, trying to force the image from her brain. "Just stop thinking about—"

Suddenly, the sound of another voice distracted her.

Amanda didn't move a muscle. She didn't breathe. She

just listened, hoping that she'd imagined what she'd heard and praying that she wouldn't hear it again.

But she did.

"Ma-maaaaaa!"

This time the sound was loud and clear as it drifted through the open window.

Amanda's heart stopped.

"Ma-maaaaaa!"

The doll that she'd left on the patio was crying out into the night!

Amanda rolled over onto her stomach and buried her head under the pillow, pretending the sound was her imagination. But even with the pillow over her head, Amanda could still hear the doll crying.

"Ma-maaaaaa!"

The cry came again. This time it was so distant and muffled, Amanda barely heard it at all.

For the next hour, Amanda lay there listening, but everything stayed quiet. At last, she drifted off to sleep.

Amanda's head was still under the pillow when she woke up the next morning. Immediately, she remembered the strange cry. She kept her head under the pillow and listened for a few minutes, but all she heard was the sound of birds singing outside.

Amanda slowly forced herself out of bed and over to the window. There was a part of her that was afraid to even look down onto the patio. Just the idea of having to look at a haunted doll sent chills up her spine. Jared was wrong. The doll didn't need a voice box to talk!

As Amanda started to pull back the curtains, she decided that her friends had to help her put the doll back in its grave—even if that meant touching it again and digging up the dead squirrel.

Amanda pulled the curtains back slowly, as if she were expecting something on the other side to jump out and say *"Boo!"* When she finally looked down onto the patio, she let out a gasp. No one had said "Boo," but the sight below her was just as startling.

CHAPTER 7

The doll was gone.

Amanda ran out of her room, down the stairs, and out the back door of the house, still dressed in her pajamas.

Maybe the doll got knocked off the table during the night, she told herself. *Maybe it's just lying on the ground somewhere, and I couldn't see it from my bedroom window.*

But even as she started to search the patio, Amanda was sure it was hopeless. Something told her that no matter how hard she looked, she was never going to find that doll. Still, she searched under every piece of furniture on the patio and crisscrossed the entire lawn twice.

She rushed back into the house to shower and dress. She could only imagine what Kevin and Laura would say when they heard that the doll really was haunted. They would freak. And wait until she told them that the doll had disappeared too. But what Amanda really wanted was to hear Jared come up with some logical explanation for what had happened. Because she certainly couldn't come up with one of her own.

Amanda stood under the spray of the shower, thinking about the doll and wondering about Barnsey. What if Kevin was right? What if Barnsey really had buried her family in the backyard?

Amanda started to shiver. Just the thought that Jared could have accidentally dug up one of Barnsey's relatives instead of the doll had Amanda in a panic.

Suddenly the shower curtain started to move. One fold after the next began to sway as if someone were brushing past it on the other side.

Amanda stood frozen under the hot water, terrified. Someone was in the bathroom with her.

That's impossible, Amanda told herself. She was sure she'd locked the door.

Still, she was too afraid to look. Finally, she forced herself to peek out from behind the curtain.

The bathroom was empty. Her pajamas were in a pile on the floor, just as she'd left them. And the door was indeed locked. But Amanda scanned the room for a few more seconds before she finally felt safe enough to let the shower curtain fall shut again.

She sighed as she stepped back under the spray. She could feel her shoulders start to relax the moment the hot water beat down on them. She was definitely alone, and safe.

But just as Amanda started washing her face, she

heard a faint squeaky sound from inside the bathroom!

She thrust her face under the stream of water and wiped the soap away from her eyes as quickly as she could. Then she pulled back the curtain to look out into the bathroom again.

Her eyes were blurry, and they stung a little from the soap, but Amanda could see that the bathroom was still empty. She was alone.

She decided that maybe that was the problem. Maybe she shouldn't be alone. She was letting herself get carried away over Barnsey and the stupid doll. She rinsed herself off quickly and turned off the water. She dried herself just as quickly and wrapped the towel around her as she stepped out of the tub.

It was then that she saw it. Amanda's body began to tremble with fear. There, right before her eyes, was positive proof that Amanda hadn't been alone at all.

CHAPTER 8

"I want my baby back!"

Amanda stood staring into the mirror above the sink. She didn't want to believe what she was seeing. Someone had written the words on the steamy mirror.

Terrified, Amanda spun around.

No one was there.

Her imagination was playing tricks on her, Amanda hoped. When she turned back to the mirror, the only thing she would see would be her own reflection.

But the words were still there.

"I want my baby back!"

Amanda blinked hard, but the words didn't go away.

She was so frightened that she could barely breathe. The bathroom suddenly felt very hot. She had to get out of there. She reached for the door knob and tried to turn it. But it didn't budge. She started twisting it more frantically, pulling on the door at the same time.

Suddenly Amanda realized that the door wouldn't open because it was still locked. But that terrified her even more. Whoever had left the message on the mirror had gotten into the bathroom without using the door! Or maybe the person had done it without coming into the bathroom at all!

There was only one person Amanda knew who had that kind of power. Barnsey!

"Oh, no!" Amanda cried out in horror. "Barnsey's put a spell on me!"

She raced into her bedroom and slammed the door shut behind her. But someone was already there, waiting for her. When Amanda bumped into a body, she started to scream.

"What's the matter with you?" Laura shouted at her.

Even when Amanda saw that it was her best friend, she couldn't control the fear. She didn't stop screaming until there was no air left in her lungs.

Just then, Amanda heard a knock. She screamed even louder.

"What in the world is going on in here?" Mrs. Peterson asked as she pushed open the door.

"Nothing, Mom." Amanda panted out the lie. There was no way she was going to tell her mother about Barnsey, because there was no way her mother would believe her. "Some creepy, crawly bug just crawled across my foot. That's all."

"Oh, for Pete's sake," Mrs. Peterson sighed. "With the way you were screaming, I thought you were being tortured up here. Could you try to keep it down a little? Your father's on the phone."

"Sorry, Mom." Amanda forced an apologetic smile.

Mrs. Peterson just shook her head as she stepped back into the hallway.

"There's no bug in here," Laura insisted, the moment Mrs. Peterson closed the door.

"I'm not really screaming about a bug!" Amanda struggled to catch her breath. "I'm screaming about Barnsey. She was just in the bathroom with me!"

"Barnsey was in your bathroom?" Laura shrieked in horror. "Why didn't you tell your mom?"

"Because I don't know if she was really in the bathroom with me," Amanda started to explain. "But she sent me a message."

"Barnsey sent you a message in the bathroom?" Laura asked.

Amanda nodded.

"What kind of a message?" Laura wanted to know.

"I'll show you." Amanda grabbed Laura's arm and dragged her out into the hallway, toward the bathroom.

"Where are we going?" Laura tried to pull her arm free.

But Amanda held tight. "You'll see."

When they got to the bathroom, she pushed Laura in ahead of her. "Look!" Amanda turned Laura so that she was facing the mirror over the sink.

"At what?" Laura asked, confused.

Amanda looked into the mirror and her heart sank. There was nothing for Laura to see but their own reflections.

The message was gone.

CHAPTER 9

"Barnsey wants that doll back," Amanda declared, convinced that that was what the message meant.

Laura sat on the edge of Amanda's bed, nodding her head in agreement.

Amanda had told Laura the whole story. She told her about the cries in the night, the missing doll, and finally, the message on the mirror.

"How are we supposed to give it back when we don't have it anymore?" Laura asked.

"We've got to find it," Amanda told her. "It's got to be out there somewhere."

But it wasn't.

"Maybe somebody took it," Laura suggested after they'd searched every inch of the yard without any luck.

"Who would have taken it?" Amanda asked hopelessly.

Laura just shrugged.

Then it came to Amanda, and she answered her own question. "My mother! That's who took it. I'll bet she threw it in the garbage."

Amanda was off and running before she even finished the sentence. She headed straight for the garbage cans that stood by the side door of the house. Sure enough, when she lifted the lid and looked inside, Amanda saw a plastic bag full of garbage.

The bag was heavy, and Amanda toppled the garbage can trying to get it out.

"I can't believe we have to dig through the garbage," Laura complained.

"Maybe we won't have to dig," Amanda said, struggling with the knot that held the bag closed. "Maybe it'll be right on top."

But they weren't that lucky. The last thing that had been thrown into the garbage bag was the remains of the previous night's dinner. There were chicken bones, mashed potatoes, and peas. And Amanda was not about to stick her hands into that mess.

"We're going to have to dump it out," she told Laura.

"Your mother will have a fit if we do that," Laura warned.

"Not if we clean it back up before she sees it." Amanda grabbed the bottom of the bag and turned it upside down.

Just then the side door opened. "Amanda!" her mother's voice shrieked. "What are you doing?" Mrs. Peterson came outside to look at the enormous mess Amanda had just made on the walkway.

"Don't worry, Mom." Amanda tried to keep her mother calm. "We'll clean it up."

Amanda's little sister had followed their mother out of the

house. "Ooooh," Casey giggled excitedly. "You're in trouble!"

Her mother ignored Casey's comment. "Why did you do this?" she asked Amanda.

"I have to find the doll," Amanda explained. "I thought you threw it away." But Amanda could already see that she'd been wrong about that. There was no doll in with the trash that was strewn on the ground at her feet.

"What doll?" Her mother was trying really hard to control her anger.

"The baby doll," Amanda answered. "The one that we dug up yesterday. I told you about it."

"I didn't throw it away," her mother assured her. "I never even saw the thing."

"I know what happened to it," Casey volunteered.

"What did you do with it, you little twerp?" Amanda demanded.

"I didn't touch it," Casey replied.

"Then where is it?" Amanda asked.

"Barnsey took it," Casey told her.

"Casey!" Mrs. Peterson scolded.

"Sorry," Casey groaned. "I mean Mrs. Barns."

"How do you know?" Amanda asked.

"I saw her do it," Casey said smugly.

"Casey, what on earth are you talking about?" Mrs. Peterson said, more as a reprimand than a question.

"Last night," Casey began her story, "when I was falling asleep, I heard a baby say 'Mama.' It was really loud. And it happened over and over again. So I got up and looked out my window. And that's when I saw Mrs. Barns. She took the doll right off the chair at the picnic table. And that made the little girl cry."

"What little girl?" Amanda asked.

"I don't know." Casey shrugged. "Just some little girl. I never saw her before."

"Maybe it was the little girl Barnsey keeps locked up in her dungeon," Laura gasped.

Amanda was thinking the very same thing. "Was the little girl all bloody and stuff, like somebody had been torturing her?" she asked Casey.

"Amanda!" Mrs. Peterson barked. "What is the matter with you? It's bad enough that you older kids make up terrible stories about Mrs. Barns, but I will not have Casey doing it too. And I will not have you filling her head with horrible notions."

"Mom," Casey protested. "I'm not making it up."

"I don't want to hear any more about it," Mrs. Peterson snapped. She took Casey by the shoulders and headed her into the house. "Come on," she said to Casey. "Let's go inside. And you two," she said over her shoulder, "clean up this mess."

Amanda and Laura began doing as they were told.

"Do you think Casey was telling the truth?" Laura asked as soon as Amanda's mother was out of earshot.

But Amanda didn't answer her. She was listening to something else, a sound she'd heard even before her mother went into the house.

"Shh," she whispered to Laura. "Listen."

Then Laura heard it too.

A deep, heart-wrenching sound that sent chills right through Amanda.

The unmistakable sound of a little girl crying was coming from Barnsey's backyard.

CHAPTER 10

"There really *is* a little girl!" Amanda gasped.

"Let's get out of here!" Laura urged.

Amanda would have liked to do just that. But she couldn't run away. The crying she heard coming from the other side of the fence was so sad, she couldn't ignore it.

"We've got to do something," she told Laura. "We've got to try and help her."

"Are you crazy?" Laura shrieked. "We'll get ourselves killed."

"No, we won't," Amanda said, trying to calm her own fears as much as Laura's. "I'm not saying that we should go rushing into Barnsey's yard. Let's just go back there and peek through the fence so we can see what's going on. Then we'll decide what to do next."

Without waiting for Laura to agree, Amanda headed for the back of the yard. Laura followed, just like she always did.

When they were halfway across the yard, the crying abruptly stopped. But Amanda kept going, with Laura right behind her. As Amanda approached the fence, her heart raced, but her feet moved slowly and cautiously. Amanda was terrified that Barnsey might be waiting on the other side of the fence to reach through the crack and grab her again. But she was determined to look anyway. She had to find out about the "little girl."

With Laura clinging to the back of her shirt, Amanda peeked through the crack into the gloomy yard on the other side. One shadow after another crept toward her as the summer breeze danced through the leaves on Barnsey's towering trees.

"Do you see her?" Laura whispered.

Amanda shook her head. Barnsey's backyard was deserted.

Laura pushed in next to Amanda to look for herself.

"What could have happened to her?" Amanda wondered aloud.

Just then, Mrs. Barns appeared from around the side of her shed. She was all dirty and carrying a big shovel.

"Look!" Laura practically screamed. "Barnsey must have buried her!"

"Shh," Amanda warned.

But it was too late. Mrs. Barns's head whirled in their direction. Amanda gasped as the woman stalked toward the fence with the shovel in her hand and an angry look on her face.

Amanda and Laura backed away. But before Amanda could turn to run, somebody grabbed her from behind.

CHAPTER 11

"Let me go!" Amanda screamed, struggling frantically against the grip that held fast around her waist.

She heard laughter close to her ear—Kevin's laughter.

"Knock it off," Jared told him.

Kevin released his grip but continued laughing. He thought he was pretty funny sneaking up on Amanda and scaring her like that.

But Amanda made him stop laughing real fast. "Barnsey's after us!" she shouted.

That was all Kevin needed to hear before he was off and running way ahead of the rest of them.

"We're in big trouble," Amanda told the boys when they reached her patio.

"What kind of trouble?" Kevin asked.

"We just saw Barnsey bury the little girl she kept in the dungeon," Laura blurted out.

"You what?" Jared practically shouted.

"We saw Barnsey bury the little girl," Laura repeated.

"Was she dead or alive?" Kevin asked, wide-eyed.

"I don't know," Laura told him.

"What do you mean, you don't know?" Kevin huffed. "Did you see the kid or not?"

"Well, not exactly," Amanda told him. "We heard a little girl crying in Barnsey's backyard. But when we went back there to look, there was no little girl. Just Barnsey carrying a big shovel."

"Then she buried her alive!" Kevin gasped.

Jared started to laugh.

"It's not funny," Laura hollered at him. "It's true!"

"Just because Barnsey had a shovel doesn't mean that she buried a little girl," Jared said. "Besides, you didn't even see a little girl, did you?"

"No," Amanda answered. "But we heard her."

"Casey saw her," Laura reminded Amanda.

"Casey!" Jared laughed even harder. "She's always making up stuff just to get attention."

"I don't think she made this up," Amanda said. "Last night, I heard the doll crying again. I didn't tell anybody about it, except Laura. But just a little while ago, Casey said she heard the doll too. And when she got up to look out her window, she saw Barnsey taking it. The little girl was with her."

"That proves there really is a little girl," Laura told the boys.

"All it proves is that Casey has a very active imagination," Jared disagreed.

"Wait a minute," Amanda said, more to herself than to

the others. "If Barnsey took the doll last night, who left the message this morning?"

"What message?" Jared asked.

"Somebody wrote a message on the bathroom mirror," Amanda told him. "It said 'I want my baby back.' At first I thought Barnsey did it. But if Barnsey already had the doll, then somebody else must have done it."

"Maybe it was the little girl," Kevin suggested.

"The little girl that Barnsey buried?" Jared asked.

Kevin nodded.

"Let me ask you a question, idiot," Jared said to Kevin. "If there really was a little girl Barnsey kept locked in the dungeon, how the heck did she get out to leave a message on Amanda's mirror?"

Kevin didn't answer.

"And if she could get out of the dungeon to go write messages," Jared continued, "how come she didn't just break out and go home?"

Kevin was stumped. "Okay, maybe it wasn't the little girl."

"And maybe Barnsey didn't take the doll either," Jared suggested.

"Maybe Jared's right," Kevin said in a tone of voice that spelled trouble. "Maybe nobody took the doll."

"What are you talking about?" Laura asked. "Somebody had to have taken that doll."

"If the doll was crying again," Kevin went on, "then it really is haunted, right?"

Amanda and Laura nodded.

"Yeah, well, maybe it's so haunted that it just walked away all by itself," Kevin told them. "Maybe it's like

Chuckie, that maniac doll in the movies who runs around trying to kill everybody! Maybe that haunted baby doll is just hiding out here waiting to do us in!"

Amanda couldn't help scanning the yard around her, terrified for a moment that maybe Kevin was right. With all that was going on, she almost expected to see the mama-screaming baby doll running at them wielding the Chuckie doll's knife.

Laura's eyes were darting about too.

"Did somebody kick you in the head when you were a baby, or what?" Jared asked Kevin, totally exasperated.

Amanda could tell that Jared didn't believe any of it. And she didn't really blame him. Listening to herself and Laura was bad enough. But listening to Kevin was like a trip to a whole new dimension. It really was all starting to sound pretty unbelievable, even to her.

"Maybe I'm just going nuts," Amanda said. It seemed to be the only explanation left that made any sense.

"That's exactly what happened to Todd French," Kevin said. "The day he got his head split open, he was following his mother into the supermarket when he felt someone tap him on the shoulder. But when he turned around to look, there was nobody there. I mean, nobody at all. But it was because Todd wasn't paying attention to where he was going that he slammed right into the door and had to be rushed to the hospital for stitches!

"And that's not the only time something like that has happened to him," Kevin continued. "Todd says he's always seeing and hearing stuff that isn't really there. It's all part of the spell. Barnsey's trying to drive him nuts. Todd's getting so desperate, he's even thinking about trying to sneak into Barnsey's house to get his cap back. And if I were you," Kevin added to Amanda, "I'd think about doing the same thing."

"What are you talking about?" Amanda demanded.

"Your bracelet," Kevin shot back. "Barnsey's got it. And you'd better figure out a way to get it back before she starts rubbing it as hard as she's been rubbing Todd French's baseball cap!"

"Oh, brother." Jared rolled his eyes. "Will you forget about Todd French? Barnsey is not trying to drive him nuts. Todd French is already nuts. And so are you," he told Kevin.

"Oh, I don't think so," Kevin said confidently. "If anybody's nuts around here, it's you. When are you going to give up and admit the truth about Barnsey?"

"When I see some proof with my own two eyes," Jared answered.

"I don't know why I even bother talking to you," Kevin told him. He walked away from Jared, shaking his head in disgust, and made his way toward the swing set on the other side of the yard.

"There really is something strange going on," Amanda said to Jared. "Maybe Kevin's right. Maybe all of this is happening because Barnsey does have my bracelet. And maybe I should be trying to figure out a way to get it back."

"You've got to stop letting Kevin get to you like this," Jared said. "I'm telling you, Todd French does not have a spell on him. And neither do you. The best thing you can do is nothing at all. I guarantee that if we just leave Barnsey alone, she'll leave us alone too."

"This has nothing to do with Kevin," Amanda said. "I know that Todd French is just a goofball. But I'm not Todd French. I know what I heard. And I know what I saw."

"Yeah," Laura chimed in. "Somebody wrote a message in the steam on the mirror while Amanda was in the shower, and the door was locked. How do you explain that?"

"You saw the message too?" Jared asked Laura.

"Well, no," Laura was forced to admit. "But Amanda did."

"I wasn't imagining it," Amanda said, trying to convince herself as much as Jared. "It really was there. And it was crystal clear too. It said 'I want my baby back.'"

Just then, Kevin called to them from the other side of the yard. He was standing near Casey's sandbox, and his voice sounded odd to Amanda. "Hey, Jared," he shouted. "You might want to bring your two eyes over here and take a look at this!"

"What now?" Jared grumbled as Amanda and Laura followed him over to the sandbox. "I'm telling you he's the only maniac running around this yard."

The moment they saw what Kevin was pointing to, Laura grabbed Amanda's shirt. Amanda could barely hold her up because her own legs were wobbling beneath her.

There, for all their eyes to see, was another message, written clearly in the sand.

CHAPTER 12

"I want my baby back—now!"

Amanda couldn't stop thinking about the message in the sandbox any more than she could stop thinking about the message on the mirror. She'd been thinking about them all day.

Jared had claimed that the writing in the sandbox was Kevin's doing, that Kevin was just trying to prove that something scary really was going on.

That might be true, Amanda thought, especially since Kevin had had such a hard time trying to keep a straight face while he denied Jared's accusations. But she didn't really know what to believe. Maybe Kevin *had* written the message in the sandbox, but he definitely hadn't written the one on the bathroom mirror. No matter how hard he'd tried, even Jared couldn't come up with a logical explanation for that.

Amanda pulled the covers up to her chin as she glanced at the clock on the nightstand beside her bed. It was already past midnight. She had been tossing and turning for over an hour trying to get to sleep.

Think of something happy, Amanda told herself as she rolled back onto her stomach, fluffing the pillow under her head again. As she squeezed her eyes shut, she tried to do just that.

It wasn't easy. It was like a Ping-Pong game going on inside her head between the happy thoughts and the horrifying ones. But after a while, the happy thoughts started to win. The nightmares of the day dissolved, and Amanda found herself drifting off into another world.

Hush, little baby, don't say a word . . .

Amanda smiled as, somewhere in the distance, a sweet voice started to sing her favorite lullaby.

Mama's gonna buy you a mockingbird . . .

Amanda listened to the song as she let herself fall deeper and deeper into sleep.

And if that mockingbird won't sing . . .

Before Amanda even realized it, she wasn't just listening, she was singing right along.

Mama's gonna buy you a diamond ring . . .

The other voice started to fade. And as the shadowy images that were dancing through Amanda's dreams began to become sharper, she found she hadn't really drifted very far at all. She was home, sitting on the swing right outside her house, singing to the most beautiful doll she'd ever seen.

Only it wasn't really Amanda's house. It was a house Amanda had never seen before, in a neighborhood that looked like a scene from an old-fashioned painting.

There were cobblestone streets lined with wrought-iron lamp posts, the kind that used gaslight. And there were funny-looking cars, cars that Amanda had seen only once before, in a black-and-white movie her father had shown her.

The clothes Amanda was wearing looked like the clothes Casey's old Raggedy Ann doll used to wear before Casey cut them up.

But the strangest thing of all was that Amanda wasn't eleven-and-a-half anymore. She was little again.

Amanda looked down at the doll she was cradling in her arms as the scent of lilacs filled the air around her.

"Anna . . ."

Amanda turned toward the sound of the voice. A woman was standing at the open screen door. She was just about the same age as Amanda's real mother. And she was just as pretty too.

"I made some lemonade. Why don't you come inside and let me pour you a glass, Anna?" the woman went on.

"Okay, Mommy." Amanda laid the doll down on the swing behind her and headed into the house.

Everything inside looked just as strange to Amanda as everything outside. But somehow it seemed totally familiar to her. As she made her way into the kitchen, Amanda seemed to know exactly where everything was, including which cabinet to open to find her favorite cup.

She stayed inside only long enough to fill her cup with lemonade. Then she headed back out to share it with her doll.

But when Amanda reached the swing, the beautiful

doll was nowhere to be seen. She started to panic.

"My baby's gone!" Amanda screamed as she dropped the cup of lemonade onto the porch. "Somebody took my baby!"

She raced back toward the front door. But before she'd made it even halfway, she saw another little girl running across the lawn—running away with her doll.

But it wasn't her doll! And it wasn't her house! And it wasn't a nice dream anymore.

"I want my baby back!" Amanda screamed as she raced down the steps of the porch and across the lawn.

The other little girl kept on going.

Amanda didn't know who the other little girl was or where she was running to. In fact, everything around Amanda started to feel a whole lot less familiar and a whole lot more frightening.

"Emily!" she screamed, suddenly knowing the other girl's name. "I want my baby back!"

But Emily didn't even turn around.

Amanda kept running. And running. And running—right out into the middle of a busy street.

"Anna! No!"

Amanda wanted to stop what was about to happen with all her heart. But it was too late. Before she could jump out of the way, she felt herself being hit head-on by a big car.

She went flying . . .

Amanda closed her eyes as tight as she could, hoping it would all go away. She didn't want to be Anna anymore! She wanted to be Amanda! And she wanted to wake up!

Just then, Amanda felt herself land—hard. When she forced open her eyes, she found herself lying at the bottom of a grave in Mrs. Barns's backyard. And Barnsey was standing over her, dumping one shovelful of dirt after another on top of her.

CHAPTER 13

Amanda could feel herself gasping for air as she struggled against the weight of the dirt piled on top of her. But she couldn't seem to move anything more than the tips of her fingers.

"Somebody help me!"

Amanda tried to scream, but the sound of her voice was so faint, it couldn't escape the walls of her grave any more than she could. Even if she screamed at the top of her lungs, no one would hear her from six feet under the moldy ground in the back of Barnsey's yard.

Barnsey had buried her alive! She was going to end up as just another scary story for Kevin to tell!

The thought of being compared to the "Lizard kid" was enough to startle Amanda right out of the grave. When she finally opened her eyes, she realized she was lying in her own bed.

The covers were way up over her head, and the sheets were tangled so tightly around her from all her tossing and turning, she was having a hard time freeing her hands.

She started to laugh at the idea that she really *was* buried alive—under her own blankets. But as she finally managed to wriggle one of her hands free and pull the covers from her face, she realized that the nightmare wasn't over at all.

Amanda wasn't just buried in blankets! She was buried in dolls!

The shelves above her bed must have fallen from the wall during the night, she thought, sending all of her dolls toppling down onto the bed.

But suddenly, as she looked up, Amanda's heart started to pound. Every one of the shelves was in place, which meant . . . someone had been in her room. Someone had piled the dolls on top of her!

Amanda sprang from her bed, terrified that Barnsey had somehow managed to creep out of her dreams in the middle of the night and into her room.

Or maybe Barnsey had sent the dolls toppling the same way she had written the message on the mirror. Maybe she was looking at Amanda right now through her evil crystal ball, laughing. And maybe she was getting ready to rub Amanda's bracelet so that something even more terrible would happen.

If Barnsey was trying to drive Amanda crazy, it was working. Amanda's head was spinning out of control.

Jared was wrong. They couldn't just "do nothing." If they didn't do something soon, Amanda really was going to end up like the "Lizard kid"!

Amanda didn't even bother to straighten up her room before she threw on her clothes and headed to the garage to grab her bike. She had to get to Jared's. She had to find a way to make him believe just how serious the situation really was. One way or another, they were going to get that bracelet back from Barnsey!

Amanda jumped on her bike and headed down the driveway at full speed. The Petersons' driveway was the steepest in the neighborhood because their house stood at the top of a big hill. In the winter, all the kids used Amanda's place as the starting point for sled races. Not only was the driveway steep, but it let out into the street right at the top of another hill that stretched all the way down to the opposite end of the neighborhood. Which was exactly where Amanda was going.

She hit the street at the end of the driveway faster than she ever had—so fast that she had a hard time keeping her feet on the pedals, which seemed to be turning all by themselves.

Amanda tried to squeeze the hand brakes to slow herself down, but before she could even get a grip on them, she was heading down Mirybrook Road, hill number two. And she was picking up even more speed.

The front tire of her bike began to shake furiously as the handlebars started to wobble. Amanda couldn't even think about trying to grab the brakes now—it was taking all of her concentration just to keep the bike steady.

It was as if someone had taken hold of the handlebars and was jerking them from side to side.

As the bike sailed down the hill, totally out of control, a desperate fear rose in Amanda's throat. Something terrible was about to take place, and she knew that Barnsey was making it happen.

CHAPTER 14

There was no way for Amanda to regain control of her bike. She was going to fall, hard, and the longer she delayed it, the worse it was going to be. The bicycle was picking up speed with every passing second.

Amanda was going to go down on her right side. She knew that when she hit the blacktop, she was going to skid. The entire side of her body would get bruised, her clothes would be torn, her skin would be scraped to shreds. She just had to remember to keep her head up, to keep her face off the ground.

Amanda tried to let go, to give in to the fall. But she couldn't. She kept fighting it, even though she knew that was a terrible mistake.

The bicycle was carrying her farther and farther away from the curb. She could hear a car coming up behind her.

Amanda didn't dare turn around to look, but she could tell that the car was getting closer. She had to get off that bike! It was the only way to stay out of the path of the car.

Amanda closed her eyes tight, shifted her weight, and braced herself for the fall.

But Amanda didn't crash onto the blacktop, as she'd expected. Instead she felt herself being lifted off the bike and floating through the air. When she opened her eyes, she realized she had landed on the ground.

Amanda was shocked. How had she landed safely on the strip of grass between the sidewalk and the curb? And how had she landed so gently that she had barely felt it?

But she didn't have much time to wonder how it happened. The sound of a blaring horn and the screech of tires startled her. The car that had been following her stopped just in time to miss her bicycle by inches.

It was a miracle. Not only had she been saved from total disaster, but she'd escaped without a scratch. As she pulled herself to her feet, Amanda felt very, very lucky.

Until she recognized the driver of the car, still stopped directly in front of her.

Barnsey!

Mrs. Barns sat in the driver's seat, staring right at Amanda. It was Barnsey who had nearly run her over.

Amanda's heart began beating wildly. Especially when Barnsey reached out to open her car door. Amanda was sure that the old woman was coming to finish her off with just her bare hands!

CHAPTER 15

"*Noooooooo!*" Amanda screamed. But as she turned to run, every muscle in her body froze. Her brain was commanding her to get away, but her body wouldn't move. She couldn't even blink. Her eyes were fixed on something even more frightening than an angry Barnsey—a little girl stood directly in front of Amanda!

The little girl smiled up at her. It was a sweet smile, friendly and innocent. But that did not ease the fear that wound itself around Amanda's heart, threatening to crush it.

The little girl who stood blocking Amanda's escape from Barnsey was not real. She was a ghost. Her clothes were bloodied and torn, and she was covered in dirt—as if she'd just climbed out of a grave.

Amanda was sure that the little girl standing in front of her was the little girl Barnsey had locked in the dungeon.

The little girl she'd buried in her backyard. Amanda was so terrified, she didn't realize she was screaming until she noticed the girl's reaction.

The child backed away from her. Her smile faded into a look of confusion. Then her lower lip began to tremble, as if she were about to burst into tears.

If only Amanda could have stopped screaming, she would have told the girl not to cry. The poor little thing was maybe seven or eight years old. And she looked so pitiful, the expression on her face just about broke Amanda's heart. There was a part of Amanda that wanted to comfort the little girl—if only she weren't a ghost!

"Amanda!" a voice called from the distance.

The ghost disappeared.

"Amanda!" It was Jared's voice, and it was much closer this time.

Amanda didn't turn toward the sound of his voice. She just continued to stare at the place where the little girl had been.

"Amanda." Jared shook her. "Are you okay?"

Amanda ignored the question and asked one of her own. "Did you see her?"

"Who?" Jared asked. "Barnsey?" He gestured toward the parked car.

Amanda had forgotten all about Barnsey. Now, as she turned toward her, she saw the woman still sitting in her car, watching Amanda with a menacing look in her eyes.

"No," Amanda answered as Barnsey put her hands on the steering wheel, and the car started slowly down the street again. "Not Barnsey. The ghost!"

Jared didn't say a word. He just looked at Amanda as if she were crazy. "Ghost," he finally managed to choke out. "Did you hit your head when you fell?" He sounded really worried. "Maybe you have a concussion."

"I didn't hit my head," Amanda told him. But she decided that there was no point in trying to convince him she'd just seen a ghost. He would never believe her.

"From what I saw, that was a pretty bad accident," Jared said.

"That was no accident," Amanda declared. "Barnsey just tried to kill me!"

"Barnsey did not try to kill you!" Jared disputed the claim as forcefully as Amanda had made it. "Barnsey did everything she could to avoid hitting you. You were the one who was all over the road."

"That's because something happened to my bike," Amanda retorted. "Something really weird. It was as if somebody grabbed the handlebars and started shaking them really hard. And there was nothing I could do to control it."

"That *is* weird," Jared agreed, heading over to inspect Amanda's bike.

Amanda followed him. "Somebody else was controlling the bike. And I know who it was. Barnsey."

Jared just shook his head, not even looking at her, as he examined the bicycle.

"I don't care what you say, Jared," Amanda went on. "Kevin's right. Barnsey has put a curse on me. I am going to end up just like the Lizard kid."

"You are not." Jared laughed. "And Barnsey has not put a curse on you. Look at this." He pointed to the place where the handlebars fit into the frame of the bicycle. "You lost a nut. Your handlebars are broken. See." He jiggled the handlebars to demonstrate. "You don't have a curse on you. In fact, you're very, very lucky. Do you have any idea how badly you could have been hurt?"

Amanda's mind flashed back to the terrible moment when she realized she had no control over the bike. "I thought I was dead," she admitted to Jared.

"Well, you're not," Jared said. "Just a little shaken up."

Amanda was a lot shaken up. She felt her body trembling all over.

"Come on," Jared said. "I'll walk you home."

Amanda walked along beside Jared as he wheeled her bike back up the hill toward her house. All she could think about was what it had felt like speeding down that hill. Her imagination was filled with one ugly picture after another of all the horrible things that might have happened.

"Don't think about it," Jared said, as if he could read her mind.

"It's hard not to," Amanda told him.

"I know," he said sympathetically. "Just keep telling yourself how lucky you are to be okay, and you'll feel a whole lot better."

Amanda tried to take Jared's advice. She tried to force all the horrible thoughts out of her head. She tried not to think about what might have been. Instead, she told herself over and over that she was lucky.

The closer she got to home, the easier it was to believe it. Amanda really was beginning to feel a whole lot better.

Until she saw what was waiting for her in the driveway.

CHAPTER 16

"IF I DON'T GET MY BABY BACK, NO ONE WILL REST IN PEACE!!!!!"

The words were written in the driveway in big block letters. Every line of every letter had been traced over and over again in different colored chalk.

Amanda could feel her insides tie themselves into a thousand knots.

What does that mean? Who isn't going to rest in peace? she wondered. *My friends and I? Or the rest of the bodies buried in Barnsey's backyard? What if they all start climbing out of their graves?*

Amanda felt as if she were going to throw up.

Jared just stood there, staring at the driveway, looking almost as unnerved as Amanda.

"Tell me I'm imagining things now," she insisted in a quivering voice.

Jared didn't answer. He reached down to touch one of

the letters. "No. You're not imagining this. It's real chalk," he said as he held his finger out to show her. "But how much do you want to bet that Kevin's clothes are covered in it?"

"What are you saying?" Amanda asked, even though she already knew the answer. "That Kevin wrote this message?"

"Yeah." Jared nodded as he wiped the pink and purple chalk from his finger onto his pants. "That's exactly what I'm saying. Kevin wrote this message, just like he wrote the message in the sandbox yesterday."

"How can you be so sure Kevin wrote the message in the sandbox?" Amanda challenged. "He swore he didn't do it."

"Oh, please." Jared laughed. "That idiot was covered in sand. The only scary thing about that message was that Kevin was actually stupid enough to sit in the sand while he wrote it."

Amanda had to laugh in spite of herself.

"Come on," Jared said as he wheeled Amanda's bike up the driveway. "He's probably up there right now trying to hide all the chalk."

Amanda followed Jared to the top of driveway, hoping that they really would catch Kevin pink- and purple-handed. But it wasn't Kevin who came walking out of the garage with a handful of chalk.

"I told you that kid would do anything for attention," Jared said as he wheeled the bike toward the garage.

"Casey!" Amanda hollered at her little sister. "Did you do this?"

"Some of it," Casey answered nonchalantly.

"What do you mean, 'some of it'?" Amanda growled.

"I mean, I did some of it!" Casey snapped back.

Amanda spun Casey around by her shoulders so she could look her straight in the face. "Did you write this or not?"

"I didn't write it," Casey said as she twisted herself out of Amanda's grip. "I just traced it in different colors after it was all done. Doesn't it look pretty?"

Amanda ignored Casey's question. She had more important things on her mind. "Do you know *who* wrote it?"

"Uh-huh." Casey nodded.

"Well, who was it?" Amanda screamed so loudly that even Jared jumped.

"Was it Kevin?" Jared asked before Casey had a chance to answer.

"Oh, puke." Casey stuck her tongue out like she was gagging. "I wouldn't color with Kevin even if he had the last piece of chalk on earth!"

"Was it Barnsey?" Amanda blurted out her worst fear.

The moment she saw the look on Casey's face, Amanda realized just how ridiculous that question was.

"Barnsey? No way!" Casey rolled her eyes. "I'd rather color with Kevin."

"You see." Jared turned toward Amanda. "Barnsey didn't leave this message."

"Neither did Kevin," Amanda pointed out. "Casey, who wrote this?"

"Anna." Casey blurted out the answer. "Anna wrote the message."

Anna?

Amanda could feel the blood draining from her face.

"Who's Anna?" Jared asked suspiciously.

Amanda's whole body started to shake. Anna was

the name of the girl in her dream the night before.

"The little girl," Casey told Jared in a huff.

Amanda grabbed Jared's arm to steady herself. "Anna is the little girl?" She could barely get the words out.

"Right." Casey nodded. "And she wants Emily to give her baby back."

"Who's Emily?" Amanda asked.

"Emily is the little girl who took Anna's baby," Casey explained.

"How do you know all this?" Amanda held her breath, waiting to hear the answer.

Casey rolled her eyes as if she'd just been asked the stupidest question in the world. "Anna told me." Casey sat down on the driveway to continue coloring.

"We've got problems even bigger than Barnsey!" Amanda told Jared.

"What are you talking about?" Jared sounded irritated as well as confused.

"Anna's the little girl!" Amanda shouted. But before she could even start to explain to Jared about her dream, Jared cut her off.

"Oh, brother," Jared huffed. "Anna is probably just another one of Casey's imaginary playmates. You know as well as I do that Casey's always making up stories about her imaginary friends. Like Zu-bi-dee-bop," Jared pointed out. "Remember him? Zu-bi-dee-bop, the giant sea serpent that lived in her closet? Maybe we ought to ask her if Zu-bi-dee-bop was coloring with her too!"

"Zu-bi-dee-bop wasn't coloring with me!" Casey screamed at Jared before Amanda had a chance to speak. "And Anna is not imaginary! She's just dead!"

CHAPTER 17

"So the little girl is really a ghost. . . ."

Amanda nodded again. She'd been over and over this a thousand times with Laura as they sat on the curb in front of Amanda's house putting on their Rollerblades. But Laura was still having a hard time taking it all in.

"And her name is Anna . . ."

"Yeah," Amanda said as she tugged at the laces of her Rollerblades. "Her name is Anna."

"Anna the ghost . . ."

Amanda started to giggle at just how silly that sounded. "Right." She laughed. "Anna the ghost."

Laura looked at Amanda as if she really was losing all her marbles. That made Amanda giggle even more.

"What's so funny?" Laura started to catch a nervous case of the giggles too.

Amanda knew that the situation wasn't funny at all.

But her brain was so fried and her nerves were so frayed that she couldn't control herself. "I just hope that Anna the ghost is as friendly as Casper the ghost," she told Laura.

Laura laughed harder. "Well, she was coloring with Casey, right?"

Amanda nodded.

"That's pretty friendly," Laura said.

"Yeah," Amanda agreed. "That's *real* friendly."

"And she saved your life, didn't she?" Laura asked seriously.

Amanda was pretty sure that Anna really had saved her life. It was the only thing that made any sense. Someone had definitely pulled her off her bike before Barnsey had a chance to run her down. And Anna the ghost was the only one who could have done it.

"Why do you think she did that?" Amanda asked as she stood up on her skates. "Why do you think she wanted to save me from Barnsey?"

Laura thought about it for a second while she tied the last knot in her laces before getting up. "Maybe she just didn't want you to end up like her," Laura said sadly.

They'd been over that a thousand times too. They'd both come to the conclusion that Anna was a ghost because Barnsey had killed her, then buried her in the backyard.

For a moment, Amanda's heart ached for Anna. There was even a part of her that wished she could see Anna again, so she could thank her for saving her life. Anna really was a friendly ghost. Amanda was sure of it.

At least until Laura opened her mouth again. "Or maybe she just doesn't want Barnsey to kill you *yet*." Laura's whole tone had changed.

"What do you mean?" Thanks to Laura, the fear began rising inside Amanda again.

"Well, Anna's the one who's been leaving all the messages, right?"

Amanda nodded.

"So Anna's the one who really wants that doll back."

"We already know all that," Amanda told Laura as they turned onto Park Drive.

"Yeah," Laura said. "But maybe Barnsey told her that *you* dug up her doll. And maybe she's really mad at you. Maybe she's so mad at you that she's going to let Barnsey kill you right after you give back her baby!"

Amanda's head was spinning as fast as the wheels on her Rollerblades. Maybe Anna really was a bad ghost. Maybe she and Barnsey were trying to drive Amanda crazy together.

Amanda struggled with the facts as she struggled to stay on her feet. And the biggest fact of all was that Amanda didn't even have Anna's baby anymore. And Anna knew it, because she had told Casey the brat that she wanted Emily to give the baby back.

"I don't have her baby," Amanda reminded Laura. "Emily has her baby."

"Yeah, right," Laura said. Suddenly something occurred to her. "What if Barnsey mowed down Emily with her car right after she ran down Anna? Maybe Barnsey buried Emily in her backyard, too, so there wouldn't be any witnesses around!"

Just then, Amanda felt herself being thrust forward. Before she could turn around and scream at Laura for pushing her, Laura started to scream herself.

Amanda was moving down the street so fast that she felt as if she were Rollerblading on a sheet of ice.

As Laura's screams got farther and farther away, Amanda braced herself against the force that was pushing her from behind—and straight toward the house that stood at 704 Shadow Lane.

CHAPTER

18

Amanda panicked and hit the brake too hard. Her feet stopped abruptly, but the rest of her body kept moving forward. She had just enough time to put her hands out in front of her to break the fall. Luckily, the pads she was wearing prevented her from getting hurt.

Laura was still screaming. Amanda knew that she was trying to say something, but her voice was so hysterical, Amanda couldn't make out any words.

She flipped herself over so that she was sitting. She was right in front of Barnsey's house, and she saw immediately what it was that had Laura so upset.

Anna the ghost had reappeared. It was Anna who had pushed Amanda down the block. But why? What did Anna want from her now? And what was she going to do next?

Amanda sat perfectly still, watching for Anna's next move.

But Anna didn't move. She just stood there, staring down at Amanda.

Amanda swallowed hard before she finally got up the nerve to speak. "I know you want your baby back." Her voice quivered as she talked to Anna. "But I don't have it anymore. So you've got to stop haunting me."

Anna shook her head no. As she took a step forward, Amanda skittered back across the grass.

"Look," Amanda yelped. "I don't know who has your doll. And I certainly don't know anybody named Emily. Believe me, if I did, I would tell her to give your doll back."

Anna turned away from Amanda and walked the few feet to the mailbox that stood at the end of Mrs. Barns's driveway. She opened the door of the mailbox and removed a stack of letters, then walked back toward Amanda and dropped the letters in Amanda's lap.

Then Anna spoke to Amanda for the first time. "You have to tell Emily to give my baby back," Anna insisted. "Or no one will rest."

With that, Anna disappeared.

"I already told you," Amanda hollered after her, knowing it was hopeless even to try. "I don't know anybody named Emily!"

But Amanda did know somebody named Emily. As soon as she looked down at the letters in her lap, she realized who it was. Amanda flipped through the letters, not wanting to believe what she saw. Every piece of mail was addressed to Mrs. Barns. Mrs. *Emily* Barns.

Barnsey didn't kill Emily! Amanda's mind was racing. *Barnsey is Emily. Somebody else must have killed Anna. But who?* Just then, her brain landed on a possible answer. *Barnsey's mother! She was probably just as evil as*

Barnsey. And she probably ran down Anna after Barnsey stole Anna's doll!

Suddenly, Laura was beside Amanda. She was still screaming. "I can't believe it!" she cried. "I saw her! I saw Anna the ghost! What did she say to you?"

Before Amanda could answer, the front door to Barnsey's house flew open and Barnsey had a question of her own. "What are you two doing there?" she snarled as she started toward the porch steps.

"Let's get out of here," Laura shrieked. With almost superhuman strength, she reached out and pulled Amanda to her feet.

"You have to tell Emily I want my baby back!"

Amanda wasn't sure whether she'd actually heard those words or whether they were just echoing in her head. Either way, it didn't matter. Amanda was not about to tell Emily Barns anything. All she wanted to do was get out of there. Fast.

"Come on!" Laura was already moving.

Just as Amanda was about to take off after Laura, her attention was drawn to all the letters strewn on the ground. Those letters were concrete proof of who Emily was, proof that Amanda wanted Jared to see with his own eyes.

Abruptly, she decided to grab one of the letters. She would return it later, after she'd shown it to Jared and Kevin.

But as Amanda bent down to take one of the letters, her skates went out from under her. A moment later, she found herself sprawled helplessly on the ground as Barnsey stalked menacingly toward her.

CHAPTER 19

Amanda scrambled to her feet with one of Barnsey's letters clutched tightly in her hand.

"Amanda! Look out!" Laura screamed.

Barnsey was just inches away. The icy, skeletal fingers that two days earlier had clamped down around Amanda's wrist were now reaching out to grab her by the back of her shirt.

Without a second to spare, Amanda took off like the wind. Her legs were pumping so hard and so fast, she blew right by Laura.

"Wait up!" Laura yelled as they turned safely off Shadow Lane.

But Amanda didn't slow down.

"She's not following us!" Laura shouted, struggling to catch up.

"I know," Amanda screamed back.

"So where are you going?" Laura puffed, grabbing her side.

"First we're going back to my house to get out of our skates, then we're going to Jared's," Amanda shouted. "Come on!"

Jared had taken Amanda's bike back to his house so that he and Kevin could fix the handlebars. As Amanda and Laura arrived at the end of Jared's driveway, they saw Jared and Kevin in the garage trying to do just that.

Amanda started waving the letter in the air as she raced toward them. But before she could even open her mouth, Laura, who was just a few feet behind, began telling the boys *her* news.

"Anna the ghost is real!" Laura squealed as she hurried up the driveway. "I saw her! With my own eyes!"

"And you're never going to believe who Emily is," Amanda jumped in before Laura took over the whole story. "Barnsey!"

"Whoa, whoa, whoa," Jared said. "What are you talking about?"

"This!" Amanda declared smugly as she shoved the letter in Jared's face. She couldn't wait to see his reaction when he saw the name "Emily Barns" on the envelope.

"What is this supposed to be?" Jared asked, as he studied the envelope.

"Look at it!" Amanda practically screamed.

"I *am* looking at it," Jared told her.

"And what does it say?" Amanda demanded.

"It says 'Occupant,'" Jared answered, sounding confused. "'704 Shadow Lane'—"

"Give me that thing," Amanda snapped impatiently as

she tugged the envelope out of Jared's hand.

It wasn't possible! She couldn't have grabbed the only letter on the ground that didn't say "Emily" on it!

But she had.

Amanda screamed in frustration the moment she saw it. "I can't believe this! This is supposed to have 'Emily Barns' written on it! This is supposed to prove to you that I'm not crazy!" she told Jared.

But the look on Jared's face told her that he definitely thought she was.

"I can't believe you risked your life for that," Laura said to Amanda. "Didn't you look at it first?"

"I didn't have time!" Amanda reminded her. "I just grabbed an envelope before Barnsey grabbed me!"

Kevin gasped. "You guys were looking through Barnsey's mail?"

"No!" Amanda shouted. "Anna the ghost threw it at me!" Amanda knew she wasn't making herself clear, but she was so upset, her mind was moving a lot faster than her tongue.

"Anna the ghost was going through Barnsey's mail?" Kevin's tongue always moved faster than *his* mind.

"She wasn't going through it," Amanda tried to explain. "She was just trying to tell me who Emily is so that she can get her baby back." Amanda's voice kept rising, right along with her anxiety. "And Emily is Barnsey! And Barnsey has the baby! And Anna wants it back! And if I don't get it for her, nobody's going to rest in peace!"

"What the heck is that supposed to mean?" Kevin asked. "Don't even tell me that the rest of Barnsey's zombie relatives are going to be climbing out of their graves to haunt us! Because I'll pack up my stuff and move out of town."

"Anna didn't say that, did she?" Laura shrieked. Kevin's panic was contagious.

But Amanda didn't answer. There were so many emotions whirling around inside her, she suddenly started to cry.

"Don't cry." Jared rushed over to comfort her. "It's okay."

"It's not okay," Amanda insisted as she wiped the tears from her face. "I have to get that doll back." She started out of the garage.

"Where are you going?" Jared asked, sounding concerned.

"To Barnsey's," Amanda told him. "I have to ask Emily to give Anna her baby back."

As Amanda headed down the driveway, she was determined to do just that.

"Wait a minute," Jared called out as he ran up beside her. "You're serious, aren't you?"

Amanda nodded. "I have to," she said. "It's the only way to put an end to this."

"Okay," Jared decided, looking as concerned as he sounded, "then we'll all go."

Amanda knew that Jared still wasn't buying the whole story, but she was grateful that he was willing to stick by her anyway.

"Come on, you guys," Jared called to Kevin and Laura. "We're going to Barnsey's."

"Oh, no!" Kevin freaked. "No way!"

Laura stood frozen.

"You don't have to come," Amanda told Laura, in the tone of voice that also said that if Laura didn't go with her, Amanda would never forgive her.

"Come on," Laura sighed as she grabbed Kevin by the arm. "If I'm going, you're going."

"Not without protection, I'm not!" Kevin said, pulling away from Laura and grabbing one of Jared's baseball bats from the corner of the garage.

"Let me ask you a question, moron," Jared huffed as Kevin and Laura came up alongside him. "Do you really think a wooden bat is enough to protect you from Barnsey? I mean, you're the guy who thinks Barnsey can blow people up on their own front lawns."

Kevin went pale. So did Laura.

Amanda knew Jared was joking, but she went pale too. Who knew what Barnsey really would do?

CHAPTER 20

"This is a very bad idea," Kevin said gravely. "Very bad."

Amanda wasn't too crazy about the plan herself, but she wasn't going to turn back now that she was here. "Let's go," she said to Jared as she took the first step onto Barnsey's driveway.

"We'll be right here if you need us," Laura called out.

"All three of us," Kevin added, tapping the baseball bat on the ground.

Amanda wasn't counting on Kevin and Laura to be much help. But if something bad really did happen, at least there would be witnesses.

"Are you as scared as I am?" Amanda asked Jared as they made their way up the driveway toward the old stone fortress that Barnsey called home.

Jared hesitated.

Amanda wanted Jared to tell her that he wasn't afraid

at all, and that there was no reason for her to be afraid either.

But Jared didn't lie. "I'm pretty scared," he admitted. Still he kept right on going.

As they climbed onto the front porch, Amanda saw the curtains move in one of the windows. Barnsey had been watching them.

"She knows we're here," Jared said.

Amanda had to fight the urge to turn and run.

"We'd better ring the doorbell before she comes out and accuses us of sneaking around out here." Jared looked for a doorbell. But there wasn't one.

"You have to knock," Amanda told him, pointing at the massive arched door that looked more like the entrance to a medieval prison than the door to a suburban house.

There was a huge brass knocker on the door. It was shaped like the head of a gargoyle. As Jared reached out for it, Amanda was afraid it might come to life and bite his hand off.

Luckily, that didn't happen. But when Jared struck the knocker against the door, the loud *bang* made Amanda jump. She could still hear the sound of the first knock echoing inside the house when Jared struck the knocker a second time.

Amanda yanked him away from the door. She didn't want either one of them standing too close when Barnsey opened it. She wasn't about to give Barnsey the chance to drag them inside. In fact, Amanda was beginning to think about running away again when the door finally creaked open.

"What do you want?" Barnsey demanded. She

glowered at them from the entrance to the dark and gloomy house.

"Hello, Mrs. Barns," Jared managed to say.

Amanda could tell by the way his voice cracked that Jared was scared half to death. It was up to Amanda to do the talking. Besides, she already knew what she was going to say.

"Mrs. Barns," Amanda started, trying to sound as polite as she could. "We've come to ask you to give back the doll."

"Doll?" Barnsey let out a cackle. "What doll?"

"The doll that was buried in my backyard," Amanda explained.

"I don't know what you're talking about." Barnsey's eyes bored through Amanda.

"Anna's doll."

At the mention of the name Anna, Barnsey stumbled as if she'd been punched. Her face went pale, and a small whimper escaped from her throat. Both hands went up to her mouth, as if to stop any other sound from escaping.

It looked to Amanda as if Barnsey might just faint dead away. For a moment, she almost felt sorry for the old woman. "Mrs. Barns, are you okay?" she asked.

Barnsey narrowed her eyes. "What kind of cruel joke are you two trying to play?" She spat out the words.

"Mrs. Barns, this is not a joke," Jared told her.

"You're right about that," Barnsey snapped back. "You get off my property. Right now. Get off my property and don't come back. Because I promise you, if I ever catch you here again, I won't give you the chance to walk away."

Then Barnsey reached out to slam the door in their faces.

A flash of metal caught Amanda's eye. She saw it for only a second before the door closed, but she knew exactly what it was. It was her friendship bracelet. And it was dangling from Barnsey's bony wrist.

CHAPTER 21

"Was she wearing Todd French's baseball cap too?"

If looks could kill, Kevin was about to fry. The glare Amanda gave him was hot enough to burn right through the bushes he and Laura were still hiding behind and blow him to smithereens.

But Laura was just as mad. "Who cares about Todd French?" she hollered as she pushed Kevin out onto the sidewalk in front of her. "Barnsey's got Amanda's bracelet!"

"No kidding," Kevin said as he turned around and pushed Laura back.

"Well, then, stop acting like such an idiot," Laura hissed. Before her fist could make contact with Kevin's stomach, Jared stepped between them.

"Cut it out, you guys!" Jared grabbed the bat away from Kevin before Kevin tried to use it.

"Yeah," Laura said, reaching around Jared to get the last licks in. "Cut it out!" She shoved Kevin hard.

"If you weren't already doomed," Kevin told Laura, "I'd cream you but good!"

"Oh, yeah?" Laura's hands went to her hips in a defiant stance. "And what's that supposed to mean?"

"*Ooooooh,* nothing." Kevin was clearly baiting the hook.

"Tell me!" Laura swallowed the bait.

"You're just doomed," Kevin taunted as he started reeling her in. "That's all."

Jared and Amanda stood staring at each other, dumbfounded. Of all the times in the world for Laura and Kevin to pick a fight, this was definitely not a good one. And it was definitely not a good place either, given the fact that they were within earshot of Barnsey's house.

"I am not doomed," Laura huffed. "Amanda's the one who's doomed!"

Amanda's jaw dropped. "Thanks for the news flash!"

Laura shrugged apologetically as Kevin just kept on reeling. "Yeah, but you're doomed even worse," he told Laura.

"Come on, Kevin, give it a rest." Jared tried to cut the line.

But Laura wouldn't let go. "No! I want him to tell me what he's saying!"

"Well, Barnsey's wearing Amanda's bracelet, right?" Laura nodded at Kevin.

"And it's the same bracelet you're wearing," Kevin pointed out smugly.

"So?" Laura rolled her eyes.

"*Sooooooo.*" Kevin rolled his eyes back at her. "That makes you best friends with Barnsey!"

Laura's eyes got so wide that Amanda was sure they were going to pop right out of her head. She knew that Kevin was just trying to torment Laura, but he definitely had a point.

"Oh, no, I'm not!" Laura yelled as she ripped her own bracelet from her wrist.

Kevin started laughing. "Oh, yes, you are!"

Without another word, Laura stormed down the sidewalk until she was directly in front of Barnsey's house. Then she wound up her arm like she was about to pitch a fastball and chucked her bracelet clear across Barnsey's front yard, onto the porch. "There you go, Barnsey," Laura screamed at the top of her lungs. "You can just be best friends with yourself!"

"Oh, man." Kevin cracked up as Laura strutted back down the sidewalk, looking prouder than a peacock. "Now she's really doomed!"

The victorious look on Laura's face began to melt the moment she saw the horrified one that was frozen across Amanda's.

"What?" Laura asked Amanda nervously.

Amanda didn't have the heart to tell Laura that the bravest action of her life was also the dumbest.

Kevin did. "I can't believe what an idiot you are," he roared. "Now all Barnsey has to do is grab the stupid thing and rub it until she rubs you to death!"

Laura turned as pale as Anna the ghost.

"You should've just stayed best friends," Kevin kept needling. "Maybe then she would have kept you alive so that she could invite you to all her rat-eating parties!"

Kevin was working Laura into such a frenzy that she

burst into tears. "I don't want to go to rat-eating parties!" Laura sobbed. "And I don't want to die either!"

"Now look what you've done, you jerk!" Amanda scolded Kevin as she tried to comfort Laura.

"Everybody just calm down!" Jared finally snapped. "Nobody's going to any rat-eating parties! And nobody's going to die either! Right, Kevin?"

Jared's tone was a warning to Kevin to back down. But Kevin refused to.

"Well, I don't know about the dying part," Kevin laughed. "But since nobody's got a bracelet, I guess nobody's going to be invited in for the rat eating."

"That's it, pal." Jared lost his temper as Laura completely lost control. "You're going up there to get that bracelet back!" He grabbed Kevin by the shirt and started pulling him down the sidewalk.

"Oh, no, I'm not!" Kevin stopped laughing as he struggled to pull away from Jared.

"Oh, yes, you are!" Jared insisted, pushing Kevin into Barnsey's front yard. "Because if you don't go up on that porch and get Laura's bracelet," he said, raising the bat over his shoulder, "I'm going to use this thing for a whole lot more than protection!"

"She's the idiot who threw it up there," Kevin hollered.

"Yeah," Amanda hollered back. "Because you made her!"

"I'm not doing it," Kevin huffed at Jared.

"Fine," Jared shot back. "Then I'll just go up there and tell Barnsey that you're the one who wants to be invited in for rat heads and milk!"

Amanda started to laugh. She knew that Jared was just

bluffing, but Kevin didn't. Before Jared could even step onto the grass, Kevin pushed him back.

"Okay, okay." Kevin panicked. "I'm going, okay?"

"Then go!"

Watching Kevin scurry across Barnsey's front lawn was a lot like watching a jack rabbit who'd just swallowed a Mexican jumping bean. He was dashing and darting, bobbing and weaving, leaping and landing all over the place.

"He's going to have a nervous breakdown before he ever hits the porch," Jared snickered as they watched Kevin bouncing from tree to tree. Finally he landed by the front steps of Barnsey's house.

Amanda didn't feel the least bit sorry for Kevin, even though she knew he was terrified beyond belief. He deserved to be terrorized after what he'd done to Laura. And Amanda was glad that Kevin was finally getting a taste of his own medicine.

Until the unthinkable happened.

"Kevin, watch out!" Amanda screamed as terror and guilt tore through her.

But the front door of Barnsey's house was already open. As Kevin reached down to grab the bracelet, Barnsey's arm was stretching out to grab him.

Her fingers wrapped tightly around the back of his T-shirt. And she wasn't letting go.

"Nooooooo!" Amanda screamed as Kevin struggled to pull himself free.

But Barnsey was pulling harder. And Amanda was sure that the old woman was pulling Kevin into the house for a whole lot more than rat heads and milk.

CHAPTER 22

It happened so quickly that Amanda couldn't believe her eyes. None of them had a chance to help Kevin because, before they could move, Kevin had already made the great escape. With one quick flick of the wrist, he had pulled his T-shirt over his head and was off and running like a shot. It was definitely a move even Houdini would have envied.

He didn't bother going down the steps. He just leaped off the porch like a superhero. His legs were pumping before he ever hit the ground. And when he did touch down, they started moving even faster. By the time he passed his friends, he was just a blur and a gust of wind.

As Kevin vanished down the street, Barnsey disappeared back into her house with Kevin's T-shirt in hand.

"You'd better go after him," Amanda told Jared. "Make sure he's okay."

"And see if he got my bracelet back," Laura added.

Jared headed off after Kevin. "You guys go back to Amanda's," he called over his shoulder. "We'll meet you there."

But when the two girls got back to Amanda's house, it wasn't Jared or Kevin who was waiting for them.

Amanda was climbing the stairs toward her room, with Laura behind her, when she heard Casey talking to someone. Amanda turned around, putting a finger to her lips to tell Laura to be quiet. Then the two of them continued creeping up the stairs as soundlessly as they could.

"How about Baby Beans?" they heard Casey say. Casey's voice was coming from her own room. "She has a bean bag body. See? You can have her."

Amanda was hoping with all her heart that Casey was talking to her imaginary sea serpent friend, Zu-bi-dee-bop. But something told her that she wasn't. And she was right.

"No, thank you, Casey," another voice answered.

It was a voice Amanda had heard only once before, but she recognized it immediately.

"Who's in there with Casey?" Laura whispered, as they reached the top of the stairs.

"Anna the ghost," Amanda answered, swallowing the lump in her throat.

Laura swallowed even harder.

"This doll's pretty cool." Casey's voice came through the open doorway again. "When you feed her a bottle, she wets her pants. Want her?"

"I don't think so," Anna answered.

Amanda and Laura snuck up to the doorway and peeked inside. There was Anna, sitting on the floor in Casey's room with her back to the door. Meanwhile, Casey was digging through her toy box, tossing out one doll after another.

"You can have any one that you want," Casey told Anna. "Really."

Amanda couldn't help thinking that the reason Anna didn't want any of Casey's dolls was that they all looked worse than the one that had been buried in the backyard. They looked even worse than Anna.

But that wasn't it at all.

"I would never take one of your babies, Casey," Anna explained. "I just want my own baby back."

"So why don't you just go to Barnsey?" Casey hesitated. "I mean Emily, and tell her to give it back."

Amanda watched as Casey sat down next to Anna as if she were any other playmate—one who just happened to be dead!

"I've tried," Anna said. "A million times. But Emily can't see me. And she can't hear me either."

"How come?" Casey asked.

"I'm not sure," Anna answered. "I think it's because her heart won't let her. She doesn't even want to think about me anymore."

"That's because Barnsey doesn't have a heart," Casey griped.

"Someone has to reach her," Anna said. Then she turned toward the open door.

Before Amanda could duck back behind the wall, Anna's eyes caught hers. It was as if Anna had known all along that Amanda was there.

"Someone has to get my baby back," Anna said, staring right into Amanda's eyes. "I will not leave without her." Then she vanished.

CHAPTER 23

It took the rest of the day, but Amanda and her friends finally came up with a plan to get the doll back. It was a dangerous plan, too dangerous to attempt in the daylight. They had to wait until after dark, when everybody else, especially Barnsey, was asleep.

Amanda arranged for Laura to spend the night at her house. That way, she could be sure that her friend wouldn't chicken out. Jared did the same thing with Kevin.

At midnight, Amanda and Laura made their way through the darkened house to the garage, where they grabbed the shovel. Then they snuck outside and headed onto the patio. Jared and Kevin were already waiting for them.

Amanda took one look at Kevin and burst into nervous laughter.

He was dressed all in black, like a cat burglar, complete with a black ski mask and black gloves. But what really made him look silly were the knee-high rubber boots he was wearing. They had bright yellow soles and were about four sizes too big for him.

"Didn't I tell you that you looked stupid?" Jared said to Kevin.

But Kevin just shrugged it off. "Hey, if I'm going to be sneaking into Barnsey's backyard, I want to make sure nobody sees me doing it."

"Then you ought to get rid of those boots," Amanda suggested. "They practically glow in the dark."

"No way," Kevin told her. "I'm wearing the boots in case I step on a rat or something."

Laura gasped.

"There are no rats in Barnsey's yard," Amanda assured her. "I was back there. Remember? And I didn't see a single rat."

"It's not rats we have to worry about," Jared reminded them. "It's Barnsey. If she catches us, we're dead."

"She's not going to catch us," Amanda said. "Look. All the lights are out in her house. She's probably sound asleep. We just have to be really quiet so she stays asleep until we find that doll."

"What if we don't find it?" Kevin asked.

"We will find it," Amanda insisted. "How many times do I have to tell you? Barnsey buried that doll behind her shed. I'm sure of it."

"What if we dig up somebody else, like one of Barnsey's other dead friends?" Kevin demanded. "Huh? What are we going to do then?"

Amanda didn't want to even think about that. In fact, she'd spent most of the night trying to convince herself and Laura that that wouldn't happen. But thanks to Kevin, everyone was panicking again.

"That's what I said!" Laura swallowed hard. "I don't want to be digging up dead bodies! Who knows what will happen to us then? I'd rather just live with Anna the ghost!"

Even Jared seemed to agree.

"Look," Amanda huffed. "According to Anna, *no one* will rest until she gets her baby back. So the bodies in Barnsey's yard might start climbing out of their graves anyway if we don't dig up that doll!"

"You don't even know for sure that the doll is really buried back there," Kevin snapped at Amanda.

"I do too," Amanda snapped back. "She's right by the shed."

"Then how come yesterday you said you were sure the little girl was buried back there?" Jared asked nervously.

"That was before we knew the little girl was a ghost," Amanda told him. "Barnsey was burying the doll," she insisted. "That's what made Anna cry."

"You'd better hope that's what happened," Jared said. "Because if Barnsey didn't really bury the doll, if she brought it inside her house, we'll never get it back."

Amanda knew that was true. Even the thought of being haunted by a yard full of ghosts for the rest of her life was not enough to make Amanda risk breaking into Barnsey's house. Not without a SWAT team anyway. "She buried it," Amanda said firmly, more to herself than to her friends.

"Then let's get this over with," Jared said. He started across the lawn carrying the same shovel he'd used the first time they dug up the doll.

Amanda followed, with Laura hanging on to her shirt. Kevin brought up the rear, clomping along in his oversized boots.

"Now remember." Jared began whispering instructions. "Stay close together. And no talking unless it's absolutely necessary. Kevin and I will look around for the spot where Barnsey was digging yesterday. Amanda and Laura, you watch our backs."

"Let's just hope nobody's back there digging already," Kevin said, "from under the earth."

They all exchanged looks.

"Do you have the flashlight?" Jared finally asked Kevin.

"Right here," Kevin answered. Then he turned it on and flashed it directly in Jared's face.

Jared's hand shot out and grabbed Kevin's arm. "Keep that thing pointed down at the ground, you moron," he whispered angrily.

They continued on in silence. The closer they got to the fence, the slower they walked. Finally they got there.

"I'll go in first," Jared whispered before any of them had a chance to have second thoughts. "Kevin, you follow me. Then Laura. Then Amanda."

Amanda knew why Jared put her last. He wanted to make sure that neither Kevin nor Laura ran away.

"Be careful," Amanda whispered, as Jared slipped through the slats and disappeared into Barnsey's yard. "Go," she said to Kevin.

"I don't know why I let you guys talk me into this," he

complained. But he followed Jared through the gap in the fence anyway.

Amanda had to push Laura through. Then she turned and took one last look at her own yard and her house. "Please don't let Barnsey catch us," she wished in a whisper. Then she slipped through the fence to join her friends.

As soon as Jared saw that they were all there, he began moving slowly toward the shed. The rest of them followed right behind. Jared had told them to stay close together, but Kevin was carrying it too far. The only way he could have gotten closer to Jared was if he climbed into his pocket. Jared kept swatting at him because Kevin kept stepping on the backs of Jared's shoes with his big, clunky boots.

Kevin kept his flashlight focused on the ground, so they could see where they were going. Amanda peered into the shadows in the direction of the old stone house. The lights were still out. Barnsey had to be asleep. But Amanda stayed alert. Her eyes had adjusted to the darkness, and she kept careful watch as they moved toward the back of the shed.

Then Amanda stumbled as her foot sank into very soft ground—ground that had recently been turned over. For a moment, she was terrified that there really was a body beneath her, digging its way out. But she didn't have a chance to tell the others—her whispers were drowned out by a louder, more insistent sound.

"Ma-maaaa!"

CHAPTER

24

The cry tore through the earth and echoed in the darkness. For a split second, Amanda had to remind herself that the sound was actually coming from the doll. The voice was so loud and so clear, it could easily have been the desperate weeping of a lost child calling out for its mother.

Amanda stepped back, relieved that they had found the spot. "She's under there," she said, pointing to the ground in front of her as she waited for Jared to start digging.

But Jared didn't move. Neither did Kevin or Laura. They just stood there, frozen, like a goofy group of horrified-looking mannequins.

"Come on, Jared." Amanda tugged at Jared's shirt to snap him out of his daze. "Dig her up so we can get out of here!"

It took a second before Jared was able to speak, but when he finally did, Amanda couldn't believe her ears.

"Maybe we should just get out of here, period!"

Amanda would have expected to hear those words from Kevin's mouth, not Jared's. But the voice of reason had been silenced by fear.

"Maybe we shouldn't be messing around with that thing at all." Jared's voice cracked as he pointed to the ground. "Who knows what'll happen! I mean, use your head, Amanda," Jared said, as forcefully as his jittery tone would allow. "That doll is really haunted!"

That was not exactly the news flash of the century. "I know the doll is haunted!" Amanda said to Jared, a whole lot louder than she had intended. "I've been telling you that since the very first day we dug her up! But I guess you had to hear her crying with your own ears before you finally believed me!"

"Shut up!" Kevin hissed as he swung the flashlight around toward Barnsey's house. "Barnsey's going to hear us! And then we'll all end up buried in a hole with that heebie-jeebie, mama-screamin' Chuckie doll!"

"Yeah, well, if you don't stop shining that thing in Barnsey's windows, she's going to see us too!" Laura hissed back as she tried to grab the flashlight from Kevin. "Give me that thing!"

"No!" Kevin refused. "I'm in charge of the flashlight!"

"Not anymore, you're not!" Laura struggled to pry the thing from Kevin's hands. As she did, the beam of light crisscrossed the sky above them as if to announce the grand opening of Barnsey's backyard.

The secret mission was definitely becoming less and

less of a secret. In fact, the four of them were causing enough commotion to wake the dead.

"If you wanted to be the flashlight guy," Kevin huffed as he yanked the flashlight from Laura's grip, "you should have said so from the beginning!"

"No!" Amanda screamed. She'd had just about enough. "I'm going be the flashlight guy!" She grabbed the flashlight away from Kevin before he saw her coming. "And you're going to shut up!" She shined the light right in Kevin's face. "And you're going to shut up too!" She moved the flashlight so that it was shining in Laura's face. "And you," Amanda spun around so that she could point the flashlight in Jared's direction, "you're going to dig!"

But before the beam of light could find its way to Jared, another face was illuminated as Anna the ghost materialized out of thin air.

"And what's she going to do?"

As usual, Kevin's mouth was working a whole lot quicker than his brain. Amanda couldn't believe that he was so mad at losing charge of the flashlight, the fact that he was seeing a ghost wasn't quite registering.

"Well, she can't dig," Laura shot back, just as mad. "She's way too little!"

"Not to mention the fact that she's a ghost!" Jared's panic-stricken voice exploded into the discussion.

Anna the ghost was registering quite nicely in Jared's brain. Amanda only wished she had a camera to capture the terrified look on his face, now that he was seeing it all with his own eyes.

The moment Jared's statement penetrated Kevin's

consciousness, he started to scream as if he were riding on the biggest rollercoaster in the entire world.

"Stop screaming!" Amanda tried to shut him up. "You're going to scare her!"

"*I'm* going to scare *her*?" Kevin got the words out with the last little bit of air that burst through his lips before he sucked in some more and started all over again.

Before Amanda could even try to calm everyone down, including Anna, the shadow of someone else was looming over them.

CHAPTER 25

As Barnsey stepped into the spotlight, terror tore through Amanda's chest like a poisonous arrow.

Amanda was trembling so badly, she had to use both hands to try and steady the flashlight. She wanted to just drop it and run, but she couldn't leave her friends behind. And she wasn't about to let Barnsey slip out of the spotlight and back into darkness, where she could attack them by surprise. If anyone was going to get the chance to make some fast moves, Amanda wanted to make sure it was going to be them.

For a second, everyone, including Anna, stood perfectly still. Even Kevin stopped screaming his head off over Anna's appearance the moment he saw Barnsey. His mouth hung wide open.

Barnsey herself stood frozen. Her small, bony body was trembling as violently as Amanda's as she stood there, glaring at them. But Barnsey wasn't shaking with fear. She was shaking with rage.

"Don't move." Barnsey's voice crackled through the air. "Don't even breathe, or, I promise, you will never live to see the light of day!"

That was all the four of them needed to hear to spring into action.

In one quick, not-so-easy maneuver, Kevin was out of his oversized, glow-in-the-dark boots and running full speed toward the fence. Jared was so close behind, *he* was practically in *Kevin's* back pocket, and Laura was right behind them.

As Barnsey took a step forward, Amanda lowered the flashlight. It was definitely time to just drop the stupid thing and run!

But as Amanda took her first step, Anna started to cry. It was a soft, muffled sound. But it was so full of sadness that Amanda couldn't hear anything else.

Amanda's head told her to keep moving. But her heart wouldn't let her. She couldn't leave that poor girl crying alone in the night, even if the girl happened to be a ghost. Amanda stopped running for her own life and turned back toward Anna.

Anna was standing between Amanda and Barnsey. "Emily," Anna sobbed. "Emily, please. You have to look at me."

"What are you doing here?" Barnsey raged. "Why do you keep tormenting me?"

For a moment, Amanda thought that Barnsey was talking to Anna. But she wasn't. Barnsey was looking right past Anna, glaring at Amanda, waiting for an answer.

Amanda was too terrified to speak. Barnsey really couldn't see Anna. She couldn't hear her either. Or if she could, she was really good at pretending not to.

Amanda could hear her friends screaming at her to run, but Anna's cries kept her right where she was.

"Emily," Anna wailed. She reached out to touch her. "Please! Please! Give my baby back!"

Suddenly, Barnsey's expression changed. She wasn't staring at Amanda anymore. She wasn't focused on anything really. Instead Barnsey had a faraway look in her eye, as if she were daydreaming about something. It looked to Amanda as if Barnsey were about to cry.

"Emily, please," Anna pleaded. "You have to look at me."

Suddenly, Barnsey's forehead crinkled into its usual scowl. As she snapped out of her daze, she wasn't looking at Anna at all. She was glaring at Amanda once more.

"I warned you what would happen if I ever caught you on my property again," Barnsey snarled maliciously.

Then she took a step forward—and walked right through Anna the ghost.

CHAPTER 26

"You'd better run while you still have the chance," Barnsey warned as she stalked toward Amanda.

But Amanda held her ground. There was no way she was abandoning Anna. "No," she told Barnsey defiantly. "I'm not leaving until you give back Anna's doll."

That stopped Barnsey dead in her tracks. "You want that doll?" she yelled at Amanda. "Fine."

The old woman picked up the shovel that Jared had dropped and started to dig.

"I'll be happy to get rid of this doll," Barnsey ranted. She wasn't really talking to Amanda. She was just rambling to herself, like a crazy person. "I wish I'd never taken it in the first place. The day I took this doll was the worst day of my life. And I have spent every minute of the past sixty-five years regretting it."

Barnsey stopped digging and bent down to pull the

doll from its grave. "Here," she shouted at Amanda. "You take it!"

Barnsey was just about to throw the doll at Amanda when something stopped her.

"Emily." Anna's voice was gentle and pleading. "Please give her back to me."

Barnsey closed her eyes tight. And when she opened them again, she wasn't looking at Amanda. She was looking straight at Anna, who was standing in front of her.

"Anna," Barnsey managed to say before she burst into tears. "Oh, Anna, is it really you?"

"Yes, Emily." Anna smiled. "It's really me."

Then Barnsey knelt down in front of the little girl so that they were face-to-face. "Oh, Anna," she cried. "I'm so sorry. I'm sorry I took your doll. I only wanted to play with her for a little while. I would have given her back . . . but I never got the chance." Barnsey's whole body shook as she began to cry even harder.

Amanda could feel tears welling up in her own eyes as she watched the scene.

"I never meant for anything bad to happen," Barnsey went on. "When I saw that car coming, I hollered for you to stop. But it was too late."

Amanda flashed back to her dream. She saw Emily running down the street with the doll. She saw the car. Then she heard the scream, "Anna! No!" It was Emily's voice she'd heard. Emily had tried to stop her.

"I would give anything to be able to change what happened to you, Anna," Barnsey said.

"You can't change the past, Emily," Anna told her. "No

one can. But you can give my baby back to me."

Barnsey picked up the doll that was resting on her lap and offered it to Anna.

The instant Anna took the doll, it began to change. In Anna's arms, the doll became beautiful. Her blue eyes sparkled. Her hair looked like silk, and her dress seemed brand-new.

"Ma-ma." This time it wasn't a cry, but a contented murmur.

Anna hugged her baby close and smiled. Then Anna began to change too. She wasn't a sad little ghost anymore. She was the most beautiful little girl Amanda had ever seen.

"Thank you, Emily," Anna said happily. "And thank you too, Amanda."

"I'm so glad you got your baby back," Amanda answered.

"Now I can rest," Anna sighed. "Now everyone can rest." With that, Anna disappeared.

Barnsey was still kneeling on the ground. She had her face in her hands and was crying as if she would never stop.

Amanda walked over to Barnsey and knelt down beside her. "Don't cry, Mrs. Barns," Amanda said soothingly, trying to hold back her own tears. She put a hand on Mrs. Barns's shoulder. "It's okay," she told her.

Barnsey looked up at Amanda. Then she wrapped her arms around her in a tight embrace, accepting her comfort.

"It's okay," Amanda repeated, holding on to Barnsey just as tightly.

From somewhere off in the distance, Anna's voice echoed that sentiment. "Don't cry, Emily. It *is* okay. It's all okay now."

•

CHAPTER 27

"Hey, Barnsey," Kevin hollered as he squeezed through the gap in the fence. "Show 'em what you've got in your pockets!"

Barnsey smiled devilishly as she reached into the front of her oversized grave-digging smock and pulled out a blood-red, slimy, slithery, squiggly, squirmy, disgusting-looking rat by its tail.

"Oh, man," Jared groaned. "That's so gross!"

"Ewwwwwww!" Laura turned away, crinkling her nose up in disgust.

"Now show them how you eat it," Kevin ordered as he stepped back into Amanda's yard, carrying Barnsey's grave-digging shovel.

Barnsey started to giggle as she lifted the rat to her mouth.

"You're not really going to do it, are you?" Jared asked, cringing at the sight.

Barnsey didn't even answer before she sank her teeth into the rat's neck and bit off its entire head.

Kevin cracked up as he and Barnsey gave each other the high-five. "I told you she loves rats!"

Barnsey winked at Amanda, then handed the rest of the gummy rat to Kevin, who immediately ripped off the tail and popped it into his mouth.

"She likes the gummy worms too," Kevin informed the group. "But the rats are her favorite."

"Only the heads, though," Barnsey reminded him.

"Yeah," Kevin laughed. "Only the heads."

"There's something seriously wrong with the two of you," Jared said as he grabbed the shovel away from Kevin.

"Hey! I'm in charge of the grave-digging shovel!" Kevin yelled as he pulled it back from Jared. "Tell him, Barnsey."

In her wildest dreams, Amanda would never have imagined the scene that was taking place around her. As she stood there in her own backyard, surrounded by her very best friends on earth, she smiled up toward the sky, hoping that Anna was somehow watching the scene as well. Because with all of her heart, Amanda was grateful to Anna the ghost for bringing their newest best friend into their lives.

Amanda's parents had been right about Mrs. Barns. She really was just a lonely old lady who didn't have any family or friends—and not because they were buried in her backyard either. Mrs. Barns explained to Amanda and the others that because she'd never gotten married, she didn't have any children of her own. And because most of her friends lived out of town, it was hard for them to visit.

Emily Barns wasn't an evil old witch! She was the coolest, funniest, nicest little old lady any one of them had ever known. And she was probably the only grown-up in the neighborhood who could tolerate Kevin. In fact, she adored Kevin as much as she adored them all. And that was almost as much as they adored her.

It all started the day after Emily gave Anna back her baby. It was almost as if Barnsey herself had been living under a spell, because when Anna finally found a way to break it, Emily Barns had become a whole new person.

Barnsey gave back all the stuff she'd taken—Amanda's and Laura's friendship bracelets, both all shiny and polished. She gave back Kevin's glow-in-the-dark boots along with a smaller pair that fit him, which she'd bought for him. And when she gave back his T-shirt, it was cleaned and pressed, with a name tag that she'd sewn on herself.

In fact, kids all over the neighborhood were getting their stuff back. Including Todd French, who was still the only kid around that Barnsey *couldn't* tolerate. She thought he was a real goofball. And Kevin had to agree. Especially when Todd fell down the sewer three days after he got his baseball cap back and six 911 trucks had to come get him out.

As the weeks went by, Barnsey did everything she could to dispel the terrible rumors that had followed her ever since Anna had died. She even started giving tours of her "dungeon," which wasn't a dungeon at all—just a regular old basement. That was a truly depressing tour for Kevin, who still wanted to believe that Barnsey was bigger than life. Barnsey promised to set up her basement like a real dungeon for Halloween, just to keep Kevin happy.

Funny how rumors always seem to start and end in the very same place, Amanda thought as she stood watching her friends.

The only thing left that no one was able to explain was the "Lizard kid." Emily said that she had never even heard of him. But she really liked hearing Kevin tell her the story over and over again.

Emily Barns was definitely their newest best friend. She even had a bracelet to prove it, a bracelet that Amanda and Laura had picked out for her because it matched theirs exactly.

The problem was, she wanted to be the shovel guy too.

"I'm in charge of the grave-digging shovel," Emily said as she pulled it from Kevin's hands.

Jared, Laura, and Amanda started to laugh. Sometimes, Kevin and Emily acted even worse than Kevin and Laura.

Besides, it wasn't really a "grave-digging" shovel. It was just a regular garden shovel. And Barnsey wasn't wearing a "grave-digging smock" either, just an apron. But Kevin still loved to tease Emily, although he couldn't bring himself to call her that. No. Kevin still fondly referred to Emily as "Barnsey," and she didn't seem to mind.

"You know, Barnsey," Kevin said, sounding irritated over having lost charge of the shovel. "You're going to have to dig a hole as big as a grave to plant that thing. You might have a heart attack or something."

"Kevin!" Laura scolded.

Emily laughed. "Don't you worry about it," she told Kevin. "I was digging holes long before you were ever born."

"Ain't that the truth," Kevin shot back.

Emily laughed even harder.

"So what am I supposed to be in charge of?" Kevin huffed.

"Supervising." Emily smiled. "Besides, it was my idea to plant it," she pointed out smugly. "So I get to dig." And with that, Emily pushed the shovel into the dirt right on top of the spot where they'd found Anna's doll.

It really was Emily's idea. Even though all four of them had gone to the nursery with her to pick it out. And all five of them had agreed upon it the moment they saw it. It was a rose bush with beautiful little pink roses that were already in bloom. It was the perfect thing for them to plant in memory of Anna. And Emily said that if they planted it in the very same spot where they'd found Anna's baby, it would always remind them of how they all came together.

"Barnsey's got a better arm than you do," Kevin told Jared as Emily pitched one shovelful of dirt after another over her shoulder.

"How much deeper do we have to go?" Laura asked Emily as she and Amanda looked on.

"Just a little deeper," Emily answered. "We need to make lots of soft dirt so the roots can breathe."

But as Emily drove the shovel back into the ground, she hit something that was anything but soft.

"Hmmm," she said as she leaned over to see what was stopping the shovel.

"It's probably a rock," Jared told her as she started to push away the dirt.

"It better be a rock," Kevin said, joking around. "And not a relative or something."

But Amanda couldn't help feeling a little bit uneasy when Emily dug into the earth again.

What *was* buried underground? she wondered.

A tinny, hard, clanking sound filled the air as Emily pushed the shovel down again.

"Oh, good heavens!" Emily knelt down and started to uncover something with her fingers. "Will you look at this?"

"What is it?" Kevin asked. "A body?"

"No." Emily giggled as she lifted an ancient, rusted jack-in-the-box from the hole she'd dug.

For a moment, Amanda thought she saw a glimmer of the old, scary Barnsey. "What is that?" she asked nervously.

"Nothing to worry about," Barnsey assured them. "Let's just say we've uncovered another ghost from the past. . . ."

Get ready for more . . .

Here's a preview of the next spine-chilling book
from A. G. Cascone

MIRROR, MIRROR

*"Mary Weatherworth." It was just a silly wishing game—
one that Lindsey and her friends had played a hundred
times before, in front of a dozen different mirrors. The
game never worked. It wasn't supposed to . . . until
Lindsey's parents brought home a strange old mirror from
an antiques auction.*

The moment Ralphie stepped inside Lindsey's room,
he practically jumped. "Geez, oh, man," he exclaimed,
staring ahead at the mirror. "What the heck is that?"

"It's a mirror, you moron," Bree shot back.

"That's what your parents bought you at the auction?"
Tommy asked, crinkling his nose.

"That thing's disgusting," Ralphie informed them.

"I know," Lindsey said. "But my mother just loves it. She says it's a valuable antique."

"You know what that means, don't you?" Ralphie didn't wait for an answer. "It means that you've got a dead person's mirror. And that's pretty *shkee-vy*."

"Tell me about it," Lindsey agreed. "You should have seen it before it was polished. It was totally creepy."

"I thought you told me this mirror was growing on you," Bree said.

"Growing like what?" Tommy asked. "A fungus?"

Just then, the seven-year-old beast came crashing into the room.

"Don't you know how to knock?" Lindsey growled at her sister, Alyssa.

"If I knocked, you'd lock the door," Alyssa replied, undeterred.

"That's the point," Lindsey said.

"I'm bored," Alyssa announced, plunking herself down on the bed. "I want to play a game or something. And Mommy said you have to."

"Look, you little dingus," Lindsey snapped. "We do not exist to amuse you. Now get out!" Lindsey went over to the door, ready to close it behind Alyssa.

Alyssa didn't budge.

Lindsey was about to start a war, but Tommy put a stop to it. "I'll play a game with you," he told Alyssa.

Lindsey rolled her eyes. Tommy was always nice to the beast. Lindsey was sure it was because Tommy didn't have to deal with a bratty little sister full-time. He was an only child.

"What do you want to play?" Tommy asked.

"How about Monopoly?" Alyssa suggested.

"No way," Lindsey jumped in. "That game takes like fifty-eight hours. Pick something else—quick."

"I know!" Alyssa exclaimed. "We can play Mary Weatherworth in Lindsey's disgusting new mirror."

"I don't think so," Ralphie said. "Mary Weatherworth is a stupid game. I'd rather play Monopoly."

Lindsey shot him a dirty look. At least Mary Weatherworth was fast. "You just don't want to play Mary Weatherworth because it totally freaks you out," she told him.

It did too. Even when they were little, Ralphie had hated anything that had to do with spirits or ghosts. In fact, he had been the only kid in kindergarten who hated Halloween—because the costumes all scared him.

"It does not," Ralphie lied.

"Does too," Tommy needled.

Bree laughed. "Ralphie's too scared to play Mary Weatherworth," she told Alyssa.

"It's just a game," Alyssa told Ralphie.

"I know it's a game," Ralphie huffed. "A dumb, stupid, moron game. But if that's what you guys want to play, fine by me."

"Go get the candle," Lindsey told Alyssa.

Five minutes later, the curtains were drawn, the candle was lit, and the chant had begun—in front of the creepy old mirror.

"Mary Weatherworth is your name.
Please appear and play this game . . ."

The candle flickered, casting eerie shadows on the strange tinted glass.

> *"For every wish we ask of you,*
> *You must make them all come true . . ."*

Lindsey, Tommy, and Bree exchanged amused glances—Ralphie already looked spooked.

> *"In return for what you give,*
> *We will let your spirit live."*

Lindsey was just about to grab Ralphie to scare him, the way she used to when they were little. But something suddenly startled *her* instead.

In fact, it startled them all.

About the Author

A. G. Cascone is the pseudonym of two authors who happen to be sisters . . . "The Twisted Sisters." In addition to DEADTIME STORIES, they have written six books, two horror-movie screenplays, and several pop songs, including one top-ten hit.

If you want to find out more about DEADTIME STORIES or A. G. Cascone, look on the World Wide Web at:
http://www.bookwire.com/titles/deadtime/

Also, we'd love to hear from you! You can write to:
A. G. Cascone
c/o Troll
100 Corporate Drive
Mahwah, NJ 07430

Or you can send e-mail directly to:
agcascone@bookwire.com

Read all of the silly, spooky, cool, and creepy

VISIT PLANET TROLL

A super-sensational spot on the Internet

at http://www.troll.com

Check out Kids' T-Zone, a really cool place where you can...

- Play games!
- Win prizes!
- Speak your mind in the Gab Lab!
- Find out about the latest and greatest books and authors!
- Shop at BookWorld!
- Order books on-line!

And a UNIVERSE more of GREAT BIG FUN!